To Lizzy,

With best wishes,

Melanie

xx

LLAMA SUTRA

LLAMA SUTRA

Melanie Whipman

InkTears
The Granary,
Purston,
Brackley,
Northants,
NN13 5PL

ISBN 978 1910207 093

British Library Cataloguing in Publication Data.
A catalogue record for this book is available from the British Library.

Typeset by Troubador Publishing Ltd
Printed and bound by CPI Group (UK) Ltd, Croydon, CR0 4YY

MIX
Paper from
responsible sources
FSC® C013604
www.fsc.org
FSC

For Dad, who gave me the key to the door.

CONTENTS

LLAMA SUTRA

The llama winks at me. The liquorice lashes of its left eye sweep down for a long second, then up again.

'Did you see that?' I nudge Simon, but his face is bent over his wrist.

'Simon.'

'What?' He taps his heart rate monitor.

'That llama, he...'

'He? You sure it's a male. Looks like a girl. They all do, don't they? Like a load of trannies. Come on. We've got to get a move on. Heart rate's down. Shouldn't have stopped at all.

'We could take a quick break, get a drink. There's a cafe.'

He steps forward, dips his hips, bends into his knee, stretches out knotted calf muscles and takes an obvious slug from his hydration system. 'You didn't have to come.'

The llama is still staring at me. He's got a shaggy, milky coat that thickens on his chest to a heavy mane. I take a step forward, my hand out. I want to touch him, to see what it feels like. His face and muzzle are a soft, ash-grey and as I move towards him he pushes his head forward and his nostrils dilate as if he's trying to smell me.

'Come on.' Simon slaps me on the backside. 'We had a deal.'

There's a strange noise, a kind of growl, a M-W-A, M-W-A, and the llama opens its mouth, flicks its head and spits at Simon. It lands on his shoulder and slides down the lycra, a fat globule of mucus.

'For Christ sake.'

I giggle.

'Get it off me.'

I tear up a fistful of grass, trying to gulp back my laughter, and wipe the gob off his shoulder. I wonder if Simon's thinking the same as me. It looks like spunk. I stop giggling and avoid his eyes.

Simon touches an ear to each shoulder, shakes out his arms and sighs. 'I'm doing this for you.'

'For us. I know.' I pull my bike from the fence and swing my leg over. Regular exercise is supposed to improve sperm count, but not cycling. Simon's had to give that up. All that tight lycra and sweaty-saddle-syndrome could damage the scrotum and threaten sperm production. He doesn't have many and they're not very motile. We found out after two years of trying. Two years of squinting at mercury, and different positions and pillows under my backside. The consultant at Clare Park was sympathetic and pragmatic, heavy fingers splayed on the desk as he leaned towards us. 'Unlikely for a natural conception, but with advances in technology there are plenty of other options...'

It was a shock. Simon only had the test to rule him out. We'd presumed it was my fault. Simon's so fit, so full of energy, so 'motile'. Now he runs and I cycle and we prepare ourselves for IVF.

Weeks of hormone injections and petroleum-gloved internals and sniffing syneral for me. Simon agrees to do my injections at home. He practises on an orange. The nurse draws a smiley face on it in black felt-tip, and then the same circle and grinning mouth high on my right buttock. I lean against the wall, weight on my left foot, right leg relaxed so my muscle isn't tensed. Simon steadies himself against my shoulder, holds the needle like a fountain pen and darts it in. It's not so bad. We've got a sense of purpose. We're working together, to a schedule, an achievable goal. When my eggs are ready for harvesting, Simon gets five minutes in a cubicle with a dog-eared porn mag and a plastic pot.

I spread my legs, and Simon and I hold hands, watching our embryos on the screen, sliding down the tube into my womb. I ease myself off the chair, terrified of gravity. They give me a photo – two little uneven circles hugged up close – which I tuck into my purse. I don't give them names, but I wish them luck, speed them on with my mind. Go numbers one and two! I yelled my head off that time Simon took me to a corporate jolly at Ascot; he's not invited me again. But now, in my mind I shout and scream: Come on numbers one and two! Hang in there. I will my womb to be warm, cosy and receptive. I listen to classical music. Lie on the sofa when I come home from work. Eat super foods.

Your body keeps you guessing – the symptoms are the same for pregnancy as your period. Sore breasts, the sensation of something shifting in your womb. I get my period before the results come through. By the time the clinic phones, my womb lining has leaked away like a strawberry-split, into the toilet and I know it's failed.

During the second cycle I'm on conference in Copenhagen. I inject myself amid the cool creams and beiges of my hotel room while everyone is networking over canapés and cava. I can't do the 'pen-hold' thing, so I grip the needle in my fist, curl my fingers tight, count to three, a quick stab in the front of my leg, the soft flesh at the top. It's surprising what you can get used to.

We're on our third attempt, when the llama spits at Simon. Our last chance. 'Fair enough,' he said, 'three's a good number.' Otherwise you could go on forever, haemorrhaging money and hope. There has to be a limit. There was a woman in the waiting room on her eighth attempt, sitting, knitting something in primrose yellow. She said they'd remortgaged the house. Some people use donor sperm, but Simon doesn't want that. And he doesn't want to adopt; he doesn't like the thought of something 'alien' in our home.

We prepare for the worst. He shows me a piece in the Sunday paper on the prohibitive cost of rearing a child. He sips his cooling coffee and folds the paper across his knees, once twice, three times, so the article is a neat, tight rectangle. £218,000 by the time they're twenty-one. It says couples are 'opting out' these days to have a better quality of living. We talk about careers and holidays and expensive hobbies.

I feel good about this third attempt. There's something special about the number three. The magic power of fairy tales. Three wishes. Third time lucky.

I go back to the llama farm. There are even more this time. A herd of push-me-pull-yous, every shade of coffee – mocha, expresso, latte, cappuccino, chocca-mocha. I recognize my one; he is the lightest – cream on the verge of burning. When he sees me he comes over, stiff-legged, high-necked. He lets me stroke him through the fence; his fur is like I imagined, as soft as the sheepskin rug I had on my bed when I was a kid. He smells of summer, of the sap of newly mown grass. He snickers into my neck, huffing on the skin of my collar bone. I wonder if he can smell my heightened hormones, sense the eggs growing inside me.

There's just a pinprick of blood on my knickers. Could be anything. Spotting, that's what they call it. It happens occasionally. Not necessarily sinister. I fold my arms across my stomach, bend over like a crumpled Coke can. 'Hang in there,' I whisper. 'Stay put, stay safe.'

Simon nods when I tell him, his face expressionless. 'Not meant to be then. Can't say we didn't give it our best shot.' He peers into the fridge, 'To tell you the truth, I always thought it was a bit unnatural.' He does that trick he used to do when we were students, of opening one beer bottle with another, levering the cap off with a sharp jerk. He takes a long slug and wipes his mouth with the back of his hand. 'Tell you what,' he says, 'Let's book a holiday.'

I find myself looking at men who look like Simon. There's a

guy on conference, same height and colouring. We chat at the bar. His fingers brush my arm to illustrate a point. I draw squiggles in the condensation on my glass and wonder if I could.

Simon buys another bike and extravagant accessories from the shop in Farnham High Street. He goes out every evening with his seven hundred quid nightlight and his new mates. They replace the lost calories with pints afterwards in lock-ins at the local pub. At home he prints out online training programmes for Iron Man competitions. His body responds obediently and at dinner parties he compares times with the other blokes. Swimming's become his forte; he powers past them all in the dark waters of Mytchett Lake, black cap gleaming, pale arms pumping and dipping.

I keep busy, I help out at the llama farm every weekend. John, the owner, is middle-aged, old-school, Barboured and Huntered, slow and deliberate. He twists a hand through hair the same chestnut as Simon's and gives a bark of laughter when I tell him about my llama spitting at my husband. 'That was just a friendly warning,' he says, 'if it wasn't green and stinky. The more riled they are, the deeper they draw their spit from. When they're really serious it's pure bile.'

One day he asks me if I want to see them mating. I'm in the back field, combing out my scorched-cream llama, my arm slung across his back, head resting against his flank. 'No hurry,' John says, 'they can last over an hour.' In the courtyard a group of llamas are milling about like grounded clouds, humming and umphing. As we approach the stable block, two youngsters come bouncing and bleating out, their hooves skittering on the cobbles. It takes a while for my eyes to adjust to the gloom. Weak sunlight filters in through a barred window and the air's thick with the dust of disturbed straw. I hear them before I see them. Soft whining and a low gargling, that makes me think of Dad on a Sunday morning in the bathroom. They're at the back of the stall. She's lying down and he's circling her, licking her ears, batting her cinnamon neck with his black one.

When he mounts her, uffing and orgling, she puts her head back, and he nuzzles and nibbles her. She closes her eyes and flicks her ears and he shifts higher, his front legs hugging her, their faces together. I press my hand to my lips, and run my fingers down my throat, trying to imagine what she's thinking. Then he's off and circling again, rubbing her neck, buzzing and whinnying and kissing and then he's astride her, humming, holding her close, clamping her tight. I lose track of time, the shadows shift and the dust flies from their coats as they bump and butt and whine. When it's over she levers herself up and they walk out together through the sun-split haze. 'The cria, the baby,' John says, 'will come in about eleven months.'

I don't tell Simon until I'm sure. Four missed periods and my low-rise jeans slipping lower and lower. I'm sick of hospitals and scans. I cancel all appointments and plan for a home birth. Simon holds me like he used to, cups my face with his hands, tells me he'll go along with anything I want. I become a cliché – I walk with the gait of a land-locked sailor, one hand soothing my stomach, the other curled into the small of my back. I feel my way into low chairs, eat odd things. Simon brings me bags of samphire from the market on the way home from work. I munch the sweet stems as if they grass.

It's a long pregnancy. Not unusual for your first, the books say. And I'm not really sure of my dates. I bring home skeins of undyed llama wool, pale and soft as chalk. Its fluffsome slipperiness is tricky to use – the needles have to be slow and steady – as I knit and purl.

My waters break at home, in the garden. I stay outside, gulping at the air, pacing and huffing and whimpering. The clouds peel apart and the sun pours down, sweet and sharp as lemonade. I kneel on the grass, in the spring sunshine, feel my body splitting open. It's all over when Simon comes home. I'm sitting on towels on the sofa, rocking my baby. She is swaddled up tight and cosy in her silky llama blanket. Simon's thoughts chase themselves across his face, then he's across the room, kissing my hair, pulling at the blanket, 'Can I..?'

I shake my head, hold her tighter, but Simon's tugging at the folds of cloth. We're pushing-pulling, pushing-pulling, and then out pops a limb and Simon yelps, and steps back, his hands covering his mouth. I fold the little cloven hoof back in.

Simon is slowly shaking his head. 'What the heck is that thing? Let me see it.'

He comes towards me and I dredge it up from deep in my gut – a mouth full of bile. I spit it at him, as hard and fast as I can.

What You'd Do For Love

Trish says, 'Let's do something interesting.' And I say, 'Cool.'

She looks at me with that little twist of a smile she has. Her head's tilted to one side and a slice of hair has slipped forward to cover half her face. On the other side, the rest of it just hangs, suspended. I want to reach out to the space between her neck and her hair and feel the shiny weight of it, as smooth and slippery as warm water against the back of my hand.

'So you're up for something?' she says, and I say, 'Like what?' very noncommittal. I can tell she's in one of her moods, she's got that fizziness about her, you can almost see the sparks flying.

'Something really interesting.' She's jigging around on the balls of her feet, one arm at her side, fingers yanking at the sleeve of her hoodie, and the other hand shivering and fisting her mouth. She's beginning to make me edgy too and I've got this dragging feeling in my stomach like someone's pulled the plug and my insides are swirling about. I yank open one side of my jacket, stick in my hand and pull out the rose. 'Da-da!'

She twists a finger through her hair and stares at it.

'Thought you'd prefer white. Red's naff, right?'

It's Mum's hobby. She gets them from the market, brings them home in a bucket on the passenger seat, strapped in safe and tight like she used to strap me in. She spends hours in the kitchen cutting

8

the stems and slicing off the thorns with Dad's old stanley knife. She lays them out in neat rows on the table, then takes them one by one, and sticks wires through the sappy wood, forces them into shape, and rams them into lumps of oasis.

I'm still holding out the rose. 'There's no thorns.'

Trish takes it from me slowly and runs a finger and thumb up the stem. 'It's weird like this. I prefer spikes.' But she slips it into her bag and the bud sticks out, kind of fat and hopeful.

'It'll open later. If you look after it. Put it in water. Or lemonade, Mum uses that sometimes to make them last longer. Something to do with the sugar. And I can get more. With thorns...'

'You're alright.' She delves into the pocket across the front of her hoodie and pulls something out. 'Look at this.'

It's as if all the stuff that was swirling about in my stomach is being sucked down the hole.

'Where d'you get it?' I can't take my eyes off it.

'Danny.'

'Right, Danny.'

'You should see your face.'

'Is it loaded?'

'Nah, don't be daft. D'you wanna hold it?'

'You're alright.'

'Come on, let's go.' She's laughing, weighing the gun in both hands.

'Let's go where?'

'You'll see. And look, I've got something else.' She drops the gun into her bag, then rummages around a bit and brings out something dark, balled up in her fist. She opens her fingers, one by one and it tumbles out, a stocking, long and black and sheer, with the foot end pointed like it's dancing.

'Like it?' She loops it around her neck and slowly tugs one end, then the other, her arms wide and her breasts pushed out. She lets me grab her and give her a snog. Her tongue's all wet and firm and minty and my stomach's liquid now and I could go on forever.

She twists her head away, 'Give us some air, Scott. Come on, let's go.'

'I love you.'

She swishes her hair back from her face and laughs, 'You're so... straight.'

It doesn't sound like a good thing when she says it. I know I'm supposed to play it cool, but I can't see the point in pretending. Carpe Diem and all that. I want to grab her and hold her tight and tell her that I'll always be straight with her, that I'll never, ever lie to her.

But this probably isn't the time. 'We could go to mine.'

'Yeah right, your mum would love that.'

'She's out. You could try them on, show me...'

'There's something I need to do first.' She screws up the stocking again, stuffs it down her top and hooks her arm through mine. 'D'you remember Grant Thompson?'

'Who?'

'Mr Thompson. Geography.'

'Not really. Didn't have him for anything.'

'He's a wanker.'

'He left, didn't he?'

'Yeah.'

We're walking down Kingston Lane, she's still got her arm looped through mine, and it feels good tucked against my side. She's not one for public affection, and it's probably only because she's cold, but it still feels nice. I squeeze it tight against my ribs and even through the layers you can feel how thin and soft it is. It's supposed to be spring but you'd never guess it, the sky's low and kind of bruised looking and it's trying to rain, that mean spitty stuff that's neither one thing or the other. The shoulder that's touching mine is the same one she's got her bag on, and it's banging, thud, thud, thud against my back with every step.

I don't know much about guns. I mean it's obviously bullets

these days, and not gunpowder or anything, so they're safe, but you still hear about them misfiring, don't you? Supposing the jolting set it off? Supposing I got shot in the back? Would that kill you? A spinal injury, paralysed, no more footie, no sex, no wanking. Mum would be feeding me with a spoon, and I'd have to listen to her yacking on forever. I knew that girl was trouble, I told you so. The whole family are trouble. You won't change her. Remember when you brought that dog home, and how it turned out, and what we had to do with it? I know you think you're helping, but some people can't be helped. She's not like you, she's been brought up with different values.

She said it wasn't loaded. But I know her. I know she doesn't always tell the truth.

We cut across the park, through the pine trees, the ground littered with pine cones, tight as grenades.

'I got him the sack.'

'What?'

'Mr Thompson.'

'How come I didn't hear about it?'

She shrugs. 'Not quite the sack. But he left because of me. We had a bit of a... he took advantage. Abused his position. I told him I'd tell. So he left.'

'Jesus, Trish.' I stop and grab her shoulder and turn her to face me. 'What happened? What did he do to you?'

She shrugs again. 'Doesn't matter. But it wasn't enough, what happened to him. It wasn't fair, what he did. I want to give him a bit of a -' she hesitates, tugging at her lower lip so I can see the inside of it, all pink and smooth and shiny, ' -a bit of a scare. I know where he lives.'

By the time we get there it's raining properly. Trish's hair has gone from straight to curly and now it's so wet it's flat against her head and with those huge eyes she makes me think of this fluffy rabbit thing I had as kid that Mum used to wash and hang on the line by it's ears, and I just want to scoop her up and keep her safe forever.

'This is it.'

It's a terraced cottage. A two up two down. The kind of house an aunt in a book would live in, with a little iron gate and a gravel path and those miniature hedges either side, that look like they've been cut with a pair of scissors.

'I don't know about this.'

'I don't know about this.' She wags her head and repeats me in a high sing-song voice. A raindrop slides down her forehead and stops at her eyebrow and it takes me back to a biology lesson a few years ago, the human body and the protective function of eyebrows. Trish was there, in the same class, sitting at a desk, next to the window. I want to ask her if she remembers how she turned and caught me staring and how, just at that moment, the sun came out and poured over her, sweet and sharp as lemonade and how she smiled back at me, all lit up. But she's looking at me like she doesn't know me so I shrug and she opens the gate and we walk through.

Our feet crunch, out of synch, my footfall just behind hers. We're making a load of noise. She stops at the porch. There's a pile of newspapers and a pair of muddy trainers with the laces still done up and a curling flier from the local church. It's the same one Mum goes to, where she does the flowers.

Trish pulls the stocking out of her top. 'Put it on.'

'You're joking, right?'

'D'you love me?'

I pull her to me, kiss her, whisper so close against her ear that I can feel the heat of my own breath. 'Yes.'

She laughs. 'Hold still.' She slips it over my head and snogs me through the stocking, our tongues warm and wet, together but separate. When she pulls away there's a tiny strand of saliva still connecting us, like the spiders' webs threading the heather together, that week when I walked my dog on the common.

'My turn.'

She pulls the other one out of her bag and puts it on, and becomes a stranger, flat-nosed and scary. I'm breathing faster and each time I inhale I smell her perfume on the nylon, sweet and spicy.

My lips feel funny when I talk, 'Look, we don't have to...We could go into town. To the pier, I've got money, I'll pay...'

'Jesus, chill out, we're only arsing about, it's a joke.' She rings the bell and pushes the gun into my hands. 'You hold it. It's more threatening from a bloke.'

It's midweek, mid-afternoon, he's probably out, working somewhere else, at another school. Maybe the one in Brighton, that was in the Times top one hundred, the one that Mum wanted me to go to. I close my eyes tight for a second, pray.

There's a noise, and I open my eyes and see movement behind the glass, and the door opens and Trish is shoving me forward, and shouting, 'You fucking wanker,' in a strange, screechy voice like Brillo on glass. And I'm stumbling into the hall, and Mr Thompson's standing there, staring, his mouth opening but not saying anything. He's mid twenties, tall, in an A&F t-shirt that's cut so it shows off the broadness of his chest and the swell of his arms. I remember him, he was good at footie, helped out with coaching sometimes. He was the sort of guy who called you 'mate' and started every sentence with 'Now here's the thing...' His skin's acne-free and he has the kind of tarty stubble on his face that always looks one day old.

Trish is jabbing at his chest, 'You changed your number. You never answered my letters.'

The wallpaper's the same embossed stuff they have in the curry house, only this has been painted white, instead of red, and there's photos of him all over. In those chunky glass clip frames. On a sailing boat, in a rugby team, his arms round his mates' shoulders, another one with his family, I suppose, at Christmas time, and one with him on a beach with some blonde girl in a bikini.

'For God's sake, Trish, this has to stop.'

It sounds wrong, him calling her Trish, as if he's her friend.

'I loved you!'

She's crying. I've seen her moody and angry and sassy, but never like this.

She rips off her stocking and her face is all blotchy and her mascara's running down her face like black blood. She's shaking her head and backing away, 'You wanker. Shoot him, Scott. Fucking shoot him!'

It's heavier than you'd think. My hands are trembling and I see my dad, before he died, with his Parkinson's, trying to hold the cup of tea I made him, with it all spilling into the saucer and onto his lap.

My stomach's in my throat.

She's never told me she loved me.

I point it at him, two handed, like in the movies. I take a breath and squeeze the trigger as tight as I can.

Click.

'You're sick,' he says. 'You need help.'

We leg it.

'Jesus, you pulled the trigger. You did it. I mean supposing it was loaded? Would you have killed him? For me?' We're on the see-saw in the park, where my Dad used to take me when I was tiny. Trish is on the high end, hair blowing, beautiful; I'm on the ground. She's got the bag in front of her, the rose still sticking out of the pocket, a bit crushed and wet, but still there.

I take a breath and swallow the lump of sick in the back of my throat, and look her in the eye. 'Don't be daft,' I say, 'Course I knew it wasn't loaded.'

BAKING BLIND

It isn't how I imagined. Three girls are bunched up on the sofa; six pale knees in a row, and five stiletto shoes scattered on the floor. One of the girls has the sixth in her hands and she's covering up the scuff marks with a black felt tip. The girls' eyes flick between the scribbling pen and the television.

When I arrived, they greeted me in English, a quick 'hi' as I stood in the living room doorway, but now they're back to their conversation, speaking in my language, but too low for me to make out all the words. Something about a party last night. One of the girls says an English phrase, and the others laugh and repeat it. It's an odd phrase – it has the sort of sound that would make you smile, with a soft 'sp' and a 'b' and two words that almost rhyme. I don't know what it means. They laugh again, and glance at me. The knot in my stomach gets tighter. It's crispy laughter, like my Mum's pies, the crust shiny and crackly, but when you dig deep it's soggy inside. I smooth my skirt, let go of the door and step into the room. 'Do you know where Barute is?' I ask.

When we were in Lithuania, Barute said there'd be pork pies, and fish and chips, and shops stocked full of designer clothes in London. He said I'd see Johnny Depp and Liam Gallagher just walking along the street. I didn't let on, but he was wasting his breath – it was the sea I was going for. When Dad was alive he had a map of Britain on his classroom wall. He took me to work once, when I was off school with glandular fever and I couldn't take another day stuck at home with Mum. I sat at the back of the class, swallowing my coughs as he spun out words I'd never heard. He was a different person there – he looked bigger – and although he still spoke softly, the English lifted his voice and all the students listened. They sat in silence, their fingers motionless on their open text-books, their faces tilted towards him. He taught me stuff at home, of course, read me English poems at bedtime, taught me how to count, but nothing like this. Mum used to tell him he was showing off. You make me feel stupid, she said. In the classroom he seemed to expand. You could feel the quiet certainty of him beneath every phrase. He was reading Shakespeare. I let his words flow round me as I stared at the poster on the wall, where Britain floated in a sea of blue, like a magic island. You'd feel safe there.

Barute was my step-dad's friend. *Kas Naujo?* he said, standing in our tiny kitchen in his flour-white shirt and shaking my Mum's hand as if she was important. I liked him, he never looked at me the way some men do, with that weight behind their eyes. He was flash – always had the latest phone, and he drove a white BMW with a fat spoiler – but he seemed comfortable here. No reason why he shouldn't; he was from the Lazdynai Estate too, a boy made good. His sister had gone to my school. Mum had spent all morning cleaning up the flat and had tried to make apple *pyragas* again. She'd never been able to cook; Dad and I used to laugh at her. She made a pie once and forgot to put the filling in, just the burnt crust and nothing inside. Barute ate his whole slice of *pyraga*, chewing and chewing the doughy pastry. He made me think of a bull I once saw at Kaunus Zoo. It stood snoozing in the dusty sun, the shadows of its muscles still under the charcoal coat, just its jaws moving in dreamy circles.

Barute nodded, smiled and washed the pie down with gulps of tea. 'You've made the right decision,' he said, raising his voice above the traffic that filtered through the gaps in the flaking window putty. 'So Laima. Fancy meeting the Queen?' And he ruffled my hair like I was six, not sixteen. Mum tugged at the hem of her best top and told him she was worried about the cost – surely renting out my room wouldn't cover the air fare. But Barute said I'd earn enough to pay him back in a month. *Nieko Tokio!* No problem, he said, laying a hand on the vee of flesh at the top of his crisp white shirt. I was a clever girl, and thanks to my father, my English was excellent.

'Yes, she's her father's daughter all right,' Mum said, 'They were like this,' she crossed one finger tightly over the other and held them up in front of her, with that silly smile. 'You should have seen them, closeted together for hours. I couldn't understand a word.'

'So her father's brains and your looks.'

She laughed, covering her mouth with the back of her hand in that gesture she has. Barute nodded and beamed. In England, he said, au-pairs were paid a lot, but with my grades and my language skills, I could name my price. I'd send money home each month and my accent would improve so much that when I came back I'd be able to walk straight into any university. He held his arms out either side of him – two doors opening wide.

It was my first time out of Lithuania, and my first trip out of Vilnius since Dad died. My heart was knocking at the bottom of my throat as I took one last look at my bedroom. I'd pulled down the Oasis and Hamlet posters, and packed away my soft toys and all my books. It looked strange and bare, as if I'd left long ago. It felt right. I was ready. Barute said it would be easier if Mum didn't come to the airport. He took my bag to the car while we said our goodbyes.

It was just the two of us. My step dad was down his local, the Namai, as usual.

'Bye then, Mum.' I touched her arm briefly and turned to go, but she lunged forwards and hugged me tight like she used to. Our bodies touched in the same places and her laughter rumbled against

17

my chest. 'You're as tall as me now. All grown up. I'm so proud of you, Laima.'

I hoped some of my friends would see me in Barute's BMW as we drove down Savanoriu Street, and over the sludgy curves of the River Neris. I inhaled leather and spicy aftershave and watched neon numbers dance on the dashboard. Barute told me what I'd need to say at the passport control in England. A holiday visiting my cousins. His signet ring tap-tapped the bottom of the steering wheel as he pulled into the traffic heading out of Lazdynai. 'For an easy life, eh. And not a lie really, you'll be staying with some other Lithuanians first. Who's to say they're not long lost relatives?'

He wrote down the address and filled in the forms as we waited on the plane, his pen bold and quick on the thin paper. The seats were narrow, and we were snugged so close his elbow jogged against my side as he wrote. He'd given me the window seat, so I had nowhere to go when the warm length of his thigh pressed mine as he helped me with my seatbelt. I caught the sweat and cigarettes beneath the aftershave as he locked me in, and then the engines roared and my stomach was left behind. Out of the window Vilnius became unreal, pocket-sized, and Barute whispered in my ear, '*Nesijaudink*. Don't worry, Goldilocks, they'll love you.' I could feel the hot huff of his breath through my hair, and when his hand cupped my head, to bring me even closer, his finger slipped into my other ear, in and out, like it was an accident.

I shifted closer to the plastic wall and closed my eyes, concentrating on the numbers in Dad's old text book. 17,820 km. That's the entire length of the British coastline. The furthest you can ever be from the sea is 113 km.

'So are you looking forward to it?' Barute pressed his hand on my leg.

Then the air hostess shoved a tray at us, and Barute was too busy struggling with cellophane seams to talk.

My English stood up to the Customs Man. When I stepped across the yellow line he held out a hand, palm up, for my passport. I didn't show off, no Shakespeare to irritate him. I understood everything he said, and when I spoke, my accent worked. 'Thank you, Sir.'

'Enjoy your holiday.' He smiled back at me.

'Thank you very much, Sir, I'm sure I will. I've been looking forward to seeing your wonderful island.'

Outside the terminal it was so bright with fake lights, you couldn't tell whether it was night or day. I took my first deep breath of English air, sniffing in dust, fumes and cigarettes. No salt. I'd thought you'd be able to smell the sea wherever you were in England. I'd imagined clean, salt-spiced air. I'd looked up the words in Dad's dictionary: saline, briny, sodium chloride. He took me to the Black Sea once. A winter's day where the sky and sea dissolved into each other. We skimmed pebbles and made drip people in the sand. When I licked my skin I tasted like a mermaid.

'You okay, Goldilocks?' Barute took my passport and we waited next to a group of huddled smokers under the sign of a smiling Pink Elephant. A black van pulled up, and Barute stepped forward. He leaned on the passenger door, his head through the window, his words too low to catch. He chucked a thumb towards the rear and I clambered in. There were benches along each wall, like the ones we had in the school gym.

'About an hour,' he said, 'give or take.' He slammed the doors and went to sit in the front, while I hung on tight at the back in the dark. There were just the tin walls, a sports bag and a white jumper with embroidered poppies crumpled on the floor.

In his classroom Dad had *The Full Works of Shakespeare*. They took up an entire shelf. I ran my fingers along their fat spines, playing at being blind as I found the indented titles. When he could no longer teach, he took one with him. Hamlet, his favourite. You'd have thought a dying man would have gone for one of the comedies, but Dad said he always liked to face his fears. Towards the end, when he had given up on the chemotherapy, he asked me to read it to him. It was just the two of us. Mum was keeping herself busy – the queues in the food shops were longer than normal, the house was dirtier than usual. She hefted furniture, shook rugs and pushed the mop into every corner. 'Come sit by me,' Dad would say, patting the bed. She'd shake her head. 'I'm making it nice, for when you're up and about.'

So I read to him, against the smell of bleach and the sound of Mum's breathing and the bucket, clinking and slopping. Even when he was dying, he couldn't stop teaching. The point of Shakespeare, he said, was that he showed us how we were all the same. He got beneath the skin, through the crust of culture, kings and common men, to the real stuff inside. He nodded, thumping his chest and wheezing out his sighing, cancerous cough. I read to him for hours. I probably didn't pronounce it right, but I liked the sound, and the rhythm reminded me of the steady shush-shush of the sea.

'Spunk bubble,' the girl in the short yellow dress says again.

It has a nice sound. I lean against the brown vinyl sofa. 'I don't know that phrase. What does it mean?'

They laugh their crispy laughs and turn their attention to the television. 'This'll help you. A few weeks of TV and your English'll be perfect.'

It's some sort of cookery show. A middle-aged Italian lady is frying onions. She is curvy and pretty and keeps licking her fingers and laughing. The rings are turning translucent in the butter, and the camera pans in so you can see how the heat softens the edges.

'Are you going to be au-pairs too?'

They avoid my eyes and reach for the cans of diet coke on the coffee table.

'Barute's got my mobile.' I gesture at the telephone on the floor in the corner of the room. 'D'you think I could...?'

'Doesn't work.'

She's lying. I've already heard it ring. The girl with the blue mascara and the waist-length hair shakes her head at me. 'Incoming calls only.'

In Lithuania they only do that if you haven't paid your bill. Perhaps Barute's been lying. Maybe it's not so easy to get a job here. Maybe that's why he's vanished.

The rasp of a key in the lock breaks the silence, then there's the sound of bolts sliding, and the slam of the front door. The girls down their cokes and push their hands into their hair, fluffing it out and cupping and smoothing the ends like Mum does.

'Daina! Ruta! Come on.' It's an English voice. His accent strangles their names.

They shove their bare feet into their identical shoes. 'Good luck.' They touch the third girl on the shoulder, a flutter of fingers, then they push past me and are gone. The felt-pen girl is left on the sofa, sitting straight and still, with her shoe in her lap. Either side of her are damp marks where the plastic stuck to her friends' four moist thighs.

It was dusk when we arrived. They opened the van doors and the air folded in, soft and cool. We were in a street of terraced houses, just like you see in English films. 'Hounslow,' Barute said. My legs had gone to sleep and I stumbled as I stepped down. Barute took my arm, tucking it through his, as if to keep me safe. It must have been raining earlier. The railings on the wall were blistered with droplets. You could see the street lights gleaming silver in the slick pavement. I closed my eyes, inhaled deeply, but couldn't smell the sea.

Two men come for the other girl and this time there's no pie crust smile. She looks as if she'd like to say something. Her mouth opens and then her hand slips up and she tugs at her lower lip. The silk

21

sleeve of her dress shifts down. For a second, I see the inside of her arm, the pale tracery of lavender veins and the needle marks freckling the tender bit in the inner dip of her elbow. It's just me and the TV-chef now. She's got a nice face and capable, floury hands. She's rolling out pastry in deft, practised strokes, and lifting the pastry across the rolling pin and into the tin. Round and round her fingers go, pushing it into the corners up to the edges, the dough pliable and unresisting. 'Firm but gentle,' she says, looking up at me. She neatens the edges with a sharp knife, twisting the tin round on her fingertips and slicing off the stuff escaping over the edge. She jabs with the fork, prick, prick. Rows of puncture marks. 'Now,' she says, 'we bake it blind. In a hot oven.'

'You ready?' It's Barute in the doorway, tall and smart in a dark suit.

My stomach turns, raw and sludgy. 'Where are we going?'

'You'll see.' He weighs his phone and cigarettes in one hand, and holds out the other to usher me towards him.

I walk away from him, to the window. I can feel him watching as I struggle with the sash catch and slide it up. Outside it is cool and moist, and across the street, I can see a phone box, a grey glass and metal thing almost invisible in the soupy air. It is not at all like I'd imagined. They are supposed to be tall and red like the photo Dad had on the classroom wall. I have some money in my pocket. Mum got me some English pounds from a friend of a friend, pressing them into my palm before I left. But I don't know whether English phone boxes take cards or cash and whether you can call a different country.

'What have you done to your hair?'

I jump. He is right next to me.

'It's just a pony tail.'

He tugs it playfully. 'It looks better down, Laima. And you want to make a good impression, don't you?'

'Okay.'

'Let me.'

He puts his phone and cigarettes on the window sill, places both palms either side of my head, squeezes gently, then slides them slowly down across my ears, to the nape of my neck where my hair is bunched with an elastic band. He tries to slip it off. It catches, and he tugs it, pulling my hair.

'Eh! Barute!' It's one of the English men, shouting from upstairs.

'What?'

'Up here. Look at this.'

Barute swears and releases my pony-tail. 'Wait here. I'll only be a sec. Sort your hair out.'

His phone is a Nokia. I look at it sitting on the window sill as I listen to his footsteps on the staircase. I used to have a Nokia, too. I would have to be very quick. I pick it up. His footsteps are above my head and there's the blurred buzz of voices, a snatched laugh. I turn it on. He is still upstairs. The screen lights up. It is taking too long. I'd forgotten the hands, reaching out for each other across the screen. They're done, and I'm pressing the numbers. I don't forget to use the international dialing code. I looked it up before I left. 370 then 5 for Vilnius. A door shuts upstairs. They are walking across the landing together. It's ringing. I check the time. Mum will be in the living room, watching the news. Perhaps she'll guess it's me as she hears it ring. She'll cup my step-father's knee as she springs up from the chair. 'It's Laima,' she'll say. He'll raise his glass at her and smile. He's not a bad man. What will I say? I can imagine the pattern of Mum's voice, how it will sound when she first hears me, and how it will change when I tell her what's happening.

'Laima?'

Her voice makes my eyes prick.

I switch off the phone and put it back carefully on the sill.

They are coming down the stairs. Barute surges into the room, head lowered. '*Paskubek*! Let's go.'

I lean right out of the window and fill my lungs with English air. I turn and smile. 'I can smell the sea.'

As I walk towards him, the television chef is opening the oven door and shoving in the pale pastry. Baking Blind. It's a funny phrase. Perhaps that's what's been wrong with Mum's pies. All those useless facts, all that time in the library and I never looked up recipes, never helped her in the kitchen. I was too much of a Daddy's girl. I wish I could tell her now. When I get home I'll show her. 'Baking Blind', I'll say in English, and she'll laugh and cover her mouth with the back of her hand in that gesture she has.

After the Flood

I can't sit still these days. Noah shakes his head and says an arse the size of mine is designed for sitting on. But I can't settle.

'I miss the ark.' I say, and he gives me that look and raps his knuckles on the side of my head, like he's trying to knock out the memories.

Noah used to miss it too. For months he walked around like a land-locked fisherman, eyes searching the horizon, legs too wide, feet ready for a tipping board. Now he strides, with the long, earth-eating gait of someone who knows he's saved the world.

Last week some bloke calls round, asking for an interview. My home-help delivers the message. She stands at the bedroom door, raises her voice so he cannot fail to hear her from the hallway, 'There's some word-monger asking for you. He's persistent.'

'Are you having a laugh?' I say, 'Aren't they all fed up with it by now? A story this old?' But I heard his voice, through the window, low and throaty, so I tell Sheila to send him down to the vineyard to find Noah. 'After lunch,' I say, 'Then he'll talk.' He likes to taste his wine with the meal. He's easy then, mellow with grape juice and a full stomach.

'No,' she says, hands fisted on her hips, mouth curved in a disgruntled rainbow, 'It's your story he wants.'

'My story?' I fiddle with the shell in my lap, hold it against my ear for a second.

'What shall I tell him then?'

I lay the conch back on the bedside table. 'That I don't do interviews, don't have a story. Nothing happened. Noah listened to God, I listened to Noah. My husband built it, loaded it, sent out the doves. I just fed the animals. Tell him to find Noah, he's the one who likes talking. And tell him to ask about the vineyard. Now there's a story. He created it, first vineyard in the world. He can see him there, taste his wine...'

Sheila's hands slip from her hips to her apron pocket, she stares at me. Through the fabric her twisting fingers look like something trapped.

'What was it like? You never say.'

If I close my eyes I can still hear it. The creaking of the timber, the slap of the water, the grunts and squeaks and whinnies and squawks. It's the silence here I find – difficult. The stillness. I have a shell in every room now, collected them one by one over the years. When I walk through the house I hold them to my ear, listen to the sea trapped inside.

'Mrs Noah?'

'I don't remember.'

I can't sit still these days, I pace and pad about this space and dream of things I shouldn't. Noah scowls and shakes his head and tells me in his soap-box-voice to quit my fidgeting. He gives me his spiel about not confusing motion with action. But there's no action for me to take, the children are long gone, there's Sheila to do the housework, and Noah tends the fertile soil of his vineyard and drinks his wine. That's what I loved about the Ark – the constant motion but no action, no decisions. We'd done all that, fifty-two years of Noah listening, and planning and chopping the cedars and building and cooking and smoking and packing the food and getting all the animals in. Then there was just the water and the waiting. A state of limbo, but for once something you didn't have to feel guilty about.

This last month Noah's changed. There's something missing. He watches my pacing in silence, his eyes clouded and cunning. I wait for his moods, those violent flashes, like a thunderstorm at sea, all threat and menace before he lashes out. But now he sits and stares at me, brooding, swollen with malice and wine. When we have sex he takes me from behind, wordless until it's over. 'Don't pretend you don't like it,' he says afterwards.

I should never have told him.

'Mrs Noah?'

He's at the gate, leaning over, eyebrows raised. I recognise the gravelly voice, the man from last week. He's disappointing in the flesh, a porridge face, too-quick to smile, one hand on the latch, the other held forward in greeting. If he had a hat he'd take it off. I look around for Sheila but it's market day.

'My husband's at the vineyard.' I don't think he is. Lately he's taken to eating meat again. He polishes his spears, goes out hunting, brings me home the bodies, feathered and furry. Dumps them on the draining board, 'Don't pretend you don't like it,' he says. This morning he was up with the first thread of birdsong. I watched him from the window, striding across to the barn in the milky dawn. His body stiff and purposeful. All action.

'I'm meeting your husband later. It's you I wanted to see. Just a few words, about your experience on the ark – as a wife. It must have been quite a journey.' He's walking up the path now, his eyes flicking past the courgettes and beans and alfalfa. 'They say you're a vegetarian?' He stands in front of me, hand shoved out, takes mine in a double-palmed clasp, like I'm some old friend. Fake idiot, but I like the way his eyes don't shift from my face when he sees the bruise.

'Just a couple of minutes,' he says.

'The water's on the boil, you can have some tea.'

'So what was it like?'

'What bit?' I look him straight in the eye, wait for him to ask how I felt leaving my family and friends behind, whether I begged Noah to save them when the rain began to fall, what I did when he stood there on the shifting deck, listening to some invisible voice, bloated with I-told-you-so's.

He runs his fingers along the grain of the table, 'Were you scared? Noah said there were storms, violent storms.'

'He hated the storms.'

'Did the animals panic?'

It was Noah who panicked. I was always ready for it, you knew when it was coming, there was that change in the air first. You'd take a breath and there'd be the sharp taste of salt, like blood, on your tongue, and a billowing blackness on the horizon, blocking out the world. You'd feel the weight of it, and the boards beginning to tip, and Noah would be all ranting fury and prayers spat out like blasphemy. 'What the fuck d'you want now? Haven't I done enough?'

I'd leave him to it, head down to the Ark's dark belly, with the animals. He'd be there waiting for me and I'd bury my face in the salty softness of his mane, hold him close until the thunder and the shrieking wind and Noah's moans were drowned out by his great rattling purr.

'Were you scared?'

'No.'

'What about the animals? What was it like living with them? They say Noah was attacked by a lion once...'

I should never have told Noah about him. I've lost my wifely arts, my feminine guile, once upon a time I'd have sealed my secret, but these days I can't keep him off my mind, off my tongue. I told him a month ago. 'Noah,' I said, not taunting or attention-seeking, but with the right degree of humbleness, real, not feigned. 'Noah, forgive me, I've sinned.'

It felt like no sin. That honeyed hide beneath my thighs and the dandelion down of his stomach. Nothing was ever so soft. You could blow it away with one whispered kiss. And the bat of his paw. Like the brush of butterfly's wings. And when I think of Noah's cuffs... Not that I have any right to complain now. What did I expect?

'On the ark, did the lion attack?'

'Noah still has the scar. He'll show you if you ask.'

It was my fault, I didn't shut the gate properly, he came up when Noah was sick with rage. It's difficult being the only man on earth, when your God is silent and every whining, shifting wind brings the keening of the dead. He leapt on top of Noah, in one great golden bound, knocked him off me. They say he has a pride now, generations of them. I imagine lazy, loose-limbed lionesses and tubby cubs stretching in the desert sun.

'I will.' He dunks his biscuit, 'I'm seeing him later,' he holds it in too long and it drops with a spongey plop into the tea.

'He knows you've come here?'

'He suggested it. He was off hunting with some friends.'

He doesn't have real friends, they hang around him, watching and waiting, seeking signs in his drunken ramblings. How do they know he won't do it all over again? Won't leave them all to drown?

The man spoons up the sludgy mess in the bottom of his cup, peers at it and pops it into his mouth. He swallows and smiles, 'Noah was heading into the desert. There's been some old lion sniffing round. Stalking the women, one by one. Just waiting and watching. Reckons it'll attack soon.'

'So I heard.'

This morning Noah came into the bedroom, told me he was

bringing me back a gift. 'Something special. You're going to love it,' he said, rattling the spears in his shoulder-pack and tugging at his beard all purpled with stale wine. I realised what was missing then – the listening. That look of perpetual distraction was gone.

'They're going to kill it,' the man gestures at the bare floor, 'It would look fine just here. Noah said he's bringing you back the pelt. A gift. I'm going to take a photo, write it up. D'you reckon it could be the same one? The one from the ark?'

I shrug and dunk my biscuit into my tea, pull it out before it falls. He found me last night, in the early hours, before Noah and the birds woke. He came through the open window in one great leap, the moon gilding his hide. I wrapped myself around him, inhaled the the hot, stinking blast of his breath, let him rest his paw on my heart, lick me head-to-toe with his coarse-moist tongue and lap away my tears.

I could have gone with him, left Noah, but I've left enough people to drown.

I pick up the shell, hold it to my ear.

'Can you hear the sea?'

I shake my head and press the shell closer, listening to the far off roar of my lion.

PEACOCK GIRL

My girl fights with a feather in her hair. Peacock blue threaded through blonde braiding. They used to eat peacocks; killed them with a feather, the quill jabbed through their brain. I found a recipe in a 1960s cookbook at the school fête. *Food through the Ages.* In the fifteenth century they cut out the bird's tongue, skinned it, oiled it, stuck it with cloves and served it to royalty.

My girl's down at Crystal Palace today. I used to watch her fight. Front row. Tasted salt when her sweat sprayed my face. Smelled the heat of her body and the tang of the oil my husband rubs into her skin. Heard her grunts and the muted clunk of glove against bone. Watched a drop of blood balloon on my jeans. On the telly it's reduced. The jabbing and darting and diving is almost balletic. Ringside, it's not like that.

Some hack from the *Argus* gave her the name when she dyed her hair blue and purple. *Our Brighton peacock struts to victory.* It stuck. The glass man in Queen's Road made her a peacock with its tail raised. He sat in the window, blowing the molten glass. We watched from outside as he puffed the life into it. Fans send her jiffy-bags fat with feathers. A seagull would have been more appropriate for our seaside town. It would have defended my girl better with its wheeling, swooping and snatching. And no one eats seagulls. She's pinned the peacock feathers to a board in her bedroom next to the posters of Cat Davis and the Webber twins.

Her room's a mess today. She left in a rush in the half-light. The curtains are still drawn, her pyjamas balled, and the duvet tangled. In the corner on the floor there's a curl of old binding, like the discarded skin of some reptile. She can only do the left hand; my husband does the right for her. He unwraps her afterwards, gentle as a woman, watching for flinching, swelling or bruising. Ice and cool towels and salves at the ready. Then he washes the wraps in a bucket in the garage.

I think of the peacock recipe as I smooth out the duvet. They stuffed the cavity with piglet, and cooked it gently, covering the neck with a damp cloth so it didn't burn. Afterwards they redressed it in its skin, the insides coated with spices, salt and cinnamon. They shoved iron up its legs and into its stomach to make it stand up straight and look alive. Finally, they filled its beak with cotton wool soaked in aquavita, set light to it, and served it breathing fire.

She left all fired up this morning. I heard their voices through the floor boards and kept my eyes closed and my breathing even when she whispered goodbye. Fight mornings, I used to wake before them, make them breakfast, but lately she leaves it cold and congealed on the plate. Says she can't eat that early. Takes a protein shake for the journey. More fabricated stuff to swell and harden her muscles. Her body's as firm as a man's. Not that I'd really know – we don't hug any more. Having a girl wasn't supposed to be like this. My friends shop with their daughters, choose eye-shadows, lipsticks, fabrics, giggle in communal changing rooms, and bond over tea and biscuits or a cheeky glass of lunchtime Sauvignon. At least, my friends say, she won't turn up pregnant.

She's always been a Daddy's girl. Watched for him coming home, forehead pressed against the glass, drawing cars and stick men in the mist of her breath. He'd toss her up and catch her, swing her round, hurl a ball at her; he'd yell instructions as she climbed the old oak on the corner. But we did stuff together too. We made ginger-bread men with raisin eyes. We iced stars to hang on the tree. And I was the one who read her to sleep.

It's a big fight today. A bout with someone from up north. Someone smaller, tighter, faster, more experienced – *the wasp*. You'd have a bet on that, wouldn't you? If you just heard their names. No contest.

They went running together last night. Just a gentle five miles. I chopped parsley and watched them from the window, high-fiving in the garden. I heard my husband tell her that she was going to win – she's faster and smarter – but to look out because the wasp's a swarmer, although her footwork's crap. I don't get involved any more. In five years she's dislocated a shoulder, fractured a hand, and two ribs, and come through the door with black eyes and split lips more times than I can remember. I stir parsley into the stew, vitamins K, C and A. Good for healing.

When I open the curtains, her medals jangle. They hang from a metal peacock stand on the windowsill. I have to fight the urge to slap the thing to the floor. It was a gift from my mother. Not condoning, she was swift to say, not taking sides. I couldn't resist it, she says, it was perfect. What's next, I say, you gonna pay for a peacock tattoo? It's a jewellery stand really, for necklaces and bangles, for girls who like to look pretty. Not such a perfect choice for her boxer-granddaughter. It's too fancy for her. All gilded metal and sparkly stones. The bird roosts safely up in a tree. The trunk broadens at the bottom for a firm base, and behind it, the bird's tail sweeps down in a studded mass of glass beads. When the sun shines it sends peacock light swirling blue and green across her room. Today it's raining. Even through the condensation you can see droplets snaking slow and blunt-nosed down the glass.

She'll want something warm tonight. Something soft in case she can't chew. I drive down to the fish market in Portslade, park in Southwick Marina and walk along Basin Road South in the drizzle, with the sea shuffling in soft and grey on my right. We used to come down here every day in the summer holidays when the weather was fine. She loved the beach when she was small, kneeling in her spotted bikini in the pools at the end of the groynes, her skin crumbed with sand, her basket heaving with weed and shrimps and crabs. I'd take a picnic of scotch eggs and carrot cake, and we'd buy vinegary cockles on polystyrene trays from the stall on the front. We'd make drip-castles, fisting out slushy sand, squeezing it, bit by bit, higher and higher to create weird and wonky towers. She never wanted to leave. Other mothers would bribe and cajole with promises of sweets at the newsagent in Southwick Square on the way home. I couldn't do that, on principle. What's the point of teaching them bribery and giving them stuff to rot their teeth? But it wasn't easy. She'd scream and wail, all snotty and red-faced, with me hissing through gritted teeth that enough was enough. In the end we struck a deal – we'd stay until our castle walls were breached. Which left us at the mercy of the tides, but sometimes you have to pick your fights.

The weather hasn't put the seagulls off today. They wheel overhead, staring with their yellow eyes, and strut fat bellied along the road in front of me as if they own it. The smell's the same as always, a mix of oil, tar, rusted metal, seaweed, fish-guts and salt. Different variations depending on the weather and season. In the fish market they wave blue-gloved hellos and greet me by name. They ask after my girl, commiserating about the bout in Brixton last month, a dubious points decision, they say. They've been out fishing half the night, battling the elements, but they smile and banter as they slice, decapitate, and flat-knife the flesh from the bone, telling me they've read about today's fight. The woman next to me tucks her whiting into a tartan wheelie bag and looks at me with her head to one side. She says she knows this girl-boxing is 'all the rage', but how can I stand it? I shrug, smile and talk about fitness and self-defence and the additional safety measures they have these days. Someone came to the school when she was ten, I say. It was me who signed the form. I don't tell her about the mother-of-all-fights we had last night.

I asked her not to go. To give it up. Enough was enough. I have a bad feeling about today, about the wasp. The fishermen wrap up my gurnard and cod, slipping in a bunch of complementary dill. A local anaesthetic, full of anti-oxidants. I nod my thanks. They wish me luck, crossing rubber fingers, slick with fish guts. She told me she loved fighting. She chucked out the usual clichés of discipline and self-esteem. She talked about the ancient Greeks, said it felt right, natural, honest. It makes me feel alive, she said. My husband stirred his pot of adrenaline chloride and vaseline with his lolly stick and kept his eyes down. I spat out the list of my dreams – detached retina, brain damage, Parkinson's, death. It sounded like a curse.

I make my way back to the car under a bruised sky and head home. No messages on the phone. I asked them not to tell me. I didn't want to know. When I google, the results aren't up. I slice the onions and peppers and fennel, sweat them in a slug of oil, add chopped chorizo, fennel seeds, garlic and chilli. Pain relief, anti-inflammatory, anti-oxidant, antibiotic. I stir in chopped tomatoes and fish stock. Omega-3s, lycopene, packed with vitamins, for bones and brains and recovery. I google again while it simmers.

I wait in the dark in her room, pressing my forehead against the window, my fingertips resting on her peacock. In my recipe book, it says peacocks are a symbol of immortality and resurrection. They guarded kings and queens in ancient times. I draw a feather in the mist of my breath. Headlights sweep the room, scatter shadows, bringing the tail beads back to life.

FALAFAL

When she sees the squashed falafal on Felicity's nightdress on Sunday evening, Marissa knows the summer is over. It has been a hot one; the sticky humidity driving the old men of Munich to visit the Englische Garten every day. Marissa has watched them over the top of Der Spiegel as they wander naked across the lawns in groups or pairs, heading slow and stiff legged towards the peppermint pools where they lower themselves on tired limbs into the cool water. She imagines the leathered creaking of their joints and wonders about their lack of self consciousness – undecided whether it shows liberation or merely the tired defeatism of age. She likes the grunts of pleasure that carry across the dry grass and ruffle the edges of her newspaper. And she likes their transformation as they kick off from the muddy bank and slip into the fluid grace of a front crawl, lapping the pond with easy, economic strokes. Afterwards they sit in a line, waist-deep, their guttural voices rising and falling, and sometimes sinking into a pool of silence that she knows is as familiar and comfortable as her own family's lazy Sunday afternoons back home in Brighton.

Whenever Marcus is very late, she considers joining them. They would welcome her, would ease aside to create room and she would sit beside them, her toes squelching in the mud. The old men would praise her German, and ask about English education and The Mortgage System. They would tell her, with nudges and winks, how they like to watch Benny Hill. She would use her best German accent, talking slowly and calmly, her past participles falling neatly at the end of each sentence, as she tells them about her grandparents and their beach hut in Worthing, with the two-ringed hob and the kettle and the English tea-bags. But the thought of Marcus's arrival always holds her back. It might coincide with her walk across the grass, his eyes might rest on her bottom and thighs, wobbling palely against her sensible black bikini, and he might see finally, who she really is.

When Marcus does come, he blocks the sun. He plucks aside her newspaper and kisses her full on the lips in front of the whole park. He is big and golden and tanned, and when he sits beside her and plays with her hair she knows that while the whole park is watching, they cannot see just how gentle his hands are as they weave and twist and plait, and brush, accidentally, the back of her neck, a whisper of a touch that echoes and tingles all the way down her spine to her toes that curl and squirm with feline delight. She wants to purr, wants to bump her head blindly against his body. He is not like everyone imagines, not really so bold and brash and confident. He can be warm and generous. He feeds her sometimes, food his Mum has cut and cooked and Tupperwared for his lunch time snack.

'I'm so glad,' he says, as he pops a fat green olive into her mouth, 'that you gave up your job.'

He's right. She should be rushing off now. For her afternoon at the Bier Kellar, changing into her crisp black and white uniform, tying back her hair, carrying out the first tray of Weizbier. She snuggles back against his chest, pushing away the series of black zeros in her Deutsche Bank passbook. 'I'll make it up next term, somehow. I can work evenings at Das Klavier.'

She asks him how his morning was at the club. He makes her laugh. Tells her tennis tales, stories of middle aged ex-pats with problem back strokes. She tries not to think of Bo Dereks and

Farrah Fawcetts, of the tennis poster of the girl and the skirt and the ball on his bedroom wall. Of his firm hands on a perfumed shoulder or on manicured fingers, solicitously correcting a grip. At least she's here and not back in England. Her Mum had kept her voice carefully casual. 'What? The whole summer? Not coming home at all? We'll miss you, but if it's important for your degree, love...'

When Marissa put the phone down she could see her Mother swallowing back her disappointment. Buck-up, she might have murmured to herself as she patted her hair in the hall mirror above the telephone. And perhaps she'd have cheered herself up by telling her neighbours over the wall, or putting out the milk bottles, telling the postman when he delivered another letter with German stamps. 'Oh no, not this summer,' she'd say, 'Marissa's staying at the university.' She'd say university like it was a foreign word. She wouldn't say 'college'. She'd tried to imitate Marissa and call it 'uni' but that's a stage too far, the ridiculousness of her own pretension made her giggle, made the word impossible to say, even to Mrs Bingley at number 43.

Marissa hasn't told Marcus's parents that she's not working anymore. She leaves each morning at the same time as Marcus. She makes the bed neatly, hospital corners on the Egyptian cotton sheet, then fluffing out the crisp duvet, and she washes and rinses her cereal bowl and coffee cup. His mother has told her not to bother, that the cleaner will do it. 'Really sweetie, there's no point.' His mother is as golden and glossy as Marcus. Sometimes the two of them go to the club together and Marcus arrives late in the Englischer Garten, still in tennis whites, smelling of Riesling and smoked salmon and his mother's heavy perfume. Marissa's tried to find a morning job, but the restaurants all want afternoon or evening staff, and she doesn't really mind her hours in the park. The summer is so perfectly glorious she feels as if the whole of Munich is holding its breath, that she is living in a dream. She sits cross legged on an old kilim that Marcus found in a cupboard in one of the spare rooms, and she listens to the German conversations around her and watches as elderly couples and young families unpack their lunches from neat parcels of greaseproof paper. As they talk they gesture with a gherkin or a rolled up circle of salami or a slice of thick, dark Shwarzbrot. She sits on her prayer rug in the shade of an oak and reads Nietsche and the Spiegel and writes her diary and letters home.

At night in the vast guest bedroom in Ringelbach Strasse she waits and waits for Marcus to come to her. When the house is finally silent, he creeps into her bedroom with cartoon stealth. Sometimes, when she hears the door creak and feels the air shift in the room, she pretends she is asleep and lies perfectly still while he tunnels in from the bottom up, whispering her name and lifting the heavy feather duvet – which is too hot for summer but comes with the guest bedroom – kissing her feet, her ankles, her shins, her knees, sliding up to lie the whole length of his warm, solid body on top of her, his weight on his elbows and his face an inch from hers. They are so close she can feel his heart, steady and even, but she can only see the shadowy outline of his head, and the thought flickers at the back of her mind, that she can't know for certain who he really is.

'I love how different you are.' He says, and as she reaches up to kiss him, a part of her registers the way he is careful to say, 'I love how...'

When he sleeps, he lies with utter abandonment, arms flung out, mouth relaxed, half-smiling. She ignores the pins and needles in her arm for fear of waking him, and watches the rise and fall of his chest and the casual flick of his pulse at the base of the neck she has just smothered with kisses. She misses their tiny square rooms at the Pfachhochschule in Reutlingen, where the neon night-time corridors are friendly and she doesn't have to trail a hand along the landing wall and worry about squeaking parquet, or whether to flush the toilet. He plays her Sade and Mark Knopfler in his room in the floor above hers and she doesn't have to wake him at 5am to send him away. She has suggested going back to the halls of residence, but Marcus tells her not to be a little idiot, that she's welcome to stay the entire holidays at his parent's house, that they don't even notice she's there.

Tonight they are having a party. The ex-pat crowd, and the tennis club, and a few of his Dad's business colleagues.

'Surely we'll be in the way.' Marissa manages, over croissants and coffee at the breakfast table. Both his parents are there and she is careful to empty her mouth of pastry and to take a sip from the thin china cup before she speaks. Marcus's father stays silent behind his paper. His mother glances up briefly from her planning list, 'Don't be silly, sweetie, of course you're to come. It's Marcus's crowd. There'll be contacts.'

Marcus concentrates on the back of his father's paper and Marissa stumbles to fill the gap but his mother stabs the air with her pen, 'And there'll be someone you know. Students, I'm sure. That girl, Felicity. From your year? Her parents are members. But if you're working...'

Marissa wonders if it's her imagination or whether her last words carry a tinge of hope. Marissa offers to help, but is rejected with smiles, there's no role left. 'No, really, sweetie, it's all sorted.' Everything has been ordered, the cleaners have been in and the house is already immaculate, vases of white lilies stand on every gleaming surface, their heavy fragrance fusing with vanilla and beeswax polish.

In the afternoon, while Marcus is giving a private lesson, Marissa washes her hair and outlines her eyes with No 7 kohl. She slips a cotton turquoise shirt over her jeans. It is Marcus's favourite. She forces herself out and finds his mother in the kitchen. Her rings and bangles sit in a neat, golden pile in the corner of the marble island, and she is kneading something in a vast china bowl, her hands squelching yolk and chickpeas and breadcrumbs. Cat Stevens whispers in the background and Marcus's mother hums along as her fingers massage the beans and egg. 'Falafals,' she says, her eyes in the bowl, 'Something I picked up during our stint in Saudi. Marcus's favourite, for now. He gets these odd fads. And the Germans are so meat obsessed, don't you think?'

Marissa stands in the doorway, heels on parquet, toes curling on flagstones. His mother glances up and smiles. 'Off you go. Go and get changed, sweetie, I'm finished here.'

After the party, in the early hours of the morning, Marcus slips beneath the duvet. He smells of wine and garlic and crawls in growling softly, with a falafal between his teeth. 'My favourite,' he says, and she's not sure whether he's speaking about her or the falafal. He feeds her with it, breaking bits off and popping them into her open mouth, stroking her cheek, kissing her hair, calling her his little sparrow, and asking her why she was so quiet, why she left the party so early. When he kisses her, she is reminded of the boxes of Negerkusse she buys from Lidl to cheer herself up when she's feeling low. Huge tea-cakes, with bitter chocolate over a mound of gooey marshmallow. Marcus's lips are full and soft too, and something in her body dissolves when his tongue touches hers. In the morning he's still there, the house is silent, snoozing gratefully from the excesses of the night before. The bars of the Georgian window are painted in sunshine and shadows across the bed and a skewed square of light has turned Marcus's hair and face to gold. She watches his eyelids flutter and when they open, she sees a moment of disorientation, just a second of confusion, that offers her a fleeting vision of school gates and a smaller Marcus in a stiff uniform. 'Sweetie,' he says, before he sneaks away, 'I'm really sorry, but you're going to have to disappear for a bit.'

A colleague of his father needs the room for an important visitor. 'Some Jap. Mix up with hotel bookings or something.' She imagines someone small and tidy, in lightweight khaki, and wonders if he'll be brave enough to request, with a polite bow, a summer duvet.

'I'm sorry,' Marcus says, grimacing, hopping on one leg to pull on his boxers, 'But you did say you could do with going back, to use the library and stuff.' He smiles and leans across to kiss her on the head. 'You're such an adorable swot, sweetie. And I'll ring every day, and you can come back as soon as we get shot of him.'

When she sees the falafal on Felicity's nightdress, the following Sunday, Marissa knows she won't be going back, and that for her, the summer is over. She has spent a week at the Reutlingen Pfachhochschule waiting for Marcus to ring. She is standing at the sink in her pyjamas, in the communal kitchen, making a bed-time drink, when Felicity comes in. Felicity's just here for one night, to collect some books, she says, to take back to her parent's place in Munich. She's seen a bit of Marcus since that fabulous party, was there for supper a couple of times, actually, and he told her to be sure to send his love. Marissa tries to keep her eyes from the tiny fleck of chick-peas on the white cotton bodice, and the circle of oil that has spread around it. She smiles and thanks her and asks if Felicity's backhand is improving.

Afterwards, sitting in her room, her hands cupped round the Snoopy mug her parents sent, Marissa tries to summon up Marcus' face, but his tanned skin and blue eyes waiver and float away. Instead she sees the cool, green shadows of the Englischer Garten and the old men, strolling past her to the pool, and the friendly flaccidity of their gently swaying penises. She regrets that she didn't join them, didn't sit under the weeping willow, waist deep in the soft, muddy water, sharing their conversation and listening to their hoarse laughter about cleavages and glace cherries, and their stories of wives waiting for them at home with a lunch they mustn't be late for. Perhaps they would have invited her.

'Bitte, bitte,' they'd have said, nodding encouragement, chuckling at their own daring. And she'd roll up her kilim as they put on their clothes and would go home with them, would be welcomed into a steamy kitchen where an aproned Frau would be stirring vats of Sauerkraut and Klopse. They'd lay an extra place for her with a crocheted doily, yellowed and worn from the frequent touch of familiar fingers. She smiles as she imagines their words.

'Machen Sie sich zu Hause,' they'd say, 'Machen Sie sich zu Hause.'

Make yourself at home.

AFTER EVER AFTER

They draw you in. Before you know it, you hear the click, click of talons on stone and the whisper of shifting feathers as they stretch and fluff, layering up the air between the millefeuilles of down. They're masters of the air. It keeps them cool, warms them and transports them. They launch themselves off my tower, rise up in the thermals, scud and tuck and leap.

I feed them every day. Tradition dictates a scattering of crumbs for the birds. The seagulls pluck them, mid-air. Their yellow lizard eyes unblinking as they snatch and gulp. The sparrows take them from my hand. The eagles are still too shy, or perhaps meat is more their thing, but what would people say if I started hurling out boar chops, venison haunches, rabbit legs?

They warn me when he comes. Before the watch-keeper rings the bells, before the gates are drawn open, before I hear his hoof beats across the courtyard, and his yelled commands and his boots hasting upon the stairs. They click and caw and peep and whine and buzz and chirp.

'Up here again?' And he takes me in his arms, leaning forward, angling me slightly, so my plait kisses the floor. 'Missed me?' my Prince asks, and I nod and smile, ignoring the discomfort of my bent spine, and trying to concentrate on his handsome face, his tanned, weather-worn skin, his slate-grey eyes. I used to liquefy at his touch, my bones melting like sugar under heat. I'd wait for him

44

every day, my body inside out with longing. Now, when he sticks his tongue in my mouth I'm reminded of the damp and writhing muscularity of the eels dropped on my tower by the sea-hawks.

'I'm thinking of cutting my hair,' I say, and he laughs and tugs it gently.

'As if. Come on, let's go down. Still can't understand why you spend so much time up here.'

'Oh, you know... habit, I guess...'

Over dinner he tells me about his day, stories of disgruntled dukes, cunning counts, plotting priests.

'Maybe tomorrow I could...?'

'Not yet, my darling Rapunzel, it's not safe out there. You'd be a target. My Achilles heel. They know I'd throw away the kingdom for you. But look...'

He claps his hands, gestures to Malik, the butler, who brings across a jewelled chest and hands it to my Prince, who passes it to me.

They are couched in a nest of purple silk, a pair of golden hand-mirrors, rimmed with rubies that glint and wink as I pick them up and twist them in my hands.

'Magic mirrors. Got them from a white witch on the docks. Marvellous things. They're made from Muranian glass. We can still be together when we're apart.'

I have heard of such things in fables and legends.

'You can see the world without ever leaving the castle, and I can watch you every minute of every day.'

'You were at the docks? I'd like to see the sea. I can smell the brine on the gulls' feathers sometimes.'

'Didn't know they came this far inland.'

I nod. 'When it's stormy.' As they wheel and dive and yowl I breathe in the salt-spiked air they carry on their feathers.

'We'll be side by side, day and night.' He cups my face with his hands and kisses me lightly on my forehead, my nose, my lips. 'I've got to go away for a few days tomorrow at first light. Off to see the Red Queen.'

'I could come with you. I could go in disguise.' I smile at him, the same smile he claims unlocked his heart. 'I could be your page-boy. Look –' I lift my hair from my face, scrape it back.

'Oh darling...'

'Wait.' I'm dipping my finger in the remains of my chocolate mousse, painting it on my upper lip. 'See. A boy. Not mousse, obviously. But a fake moustache of some sort. Malik – you'll think of something, won't you?'

My Prince shakes his head and laughs, and pulls me to him, kisses and licks and sucks away the chocolate. 'Now don't be silly, darling.'

I find myself wanting to pout, to stamp my foot, to scream. I'm not that kind of girl. I lived in the witch's tower for five years and kept my sanity; I sang every day until the Prince came; it was me who fought and killed her when she tricked us, it was me who found my thorn-blinded Prince; it was me who bathed his damaged eyes back to life. Now I see no one but the staff. He fears for my life. Dogs and soldiers patrol the gardens. There are huge signs on the gates. Private. No hawkers, no salesmen or women. He scours the papers for tales to justify his fears. He comes home with stories of witches disguised as travelling saleswomen. Hair combs spiked with poison, apples that kill, belts that tighten and suffocate.

'How about a song?' he says.

'Not tonight.'

'A game of snap?'

'I was thinking of buying a loom.'

'A loom?'

I watch his thoughts chase themselves across his face; he runs his finger and thumb along his jawline, and pinches them together at the base of his handsome cleft chin. He's not hard to read. I asked for a spinning wheel first, and he shook his head and reminded me of that dreadful case in the next kingdom. A princess in a coma and cut off from life after one prick from a dusty needle. I wanted to take up gardening, but he showed me a newspaper article about roses that grew up to engulf a castle, and a rose bush that lured a father to betray his daughter to a beast. He showed me pages of poisonous plants, deadly nightshades and foxgloves and beans that twine themselves up into lands of giants... I took him into the kitchens and asked for cooking lessons and he looked in horror at the knives bristling from their block, and at the huge iron oven, and he spun some nonsense about a Gingerbread Man that came to life. I even asked for dancing lessons. Surely there could be no hidden dangers there – that's what princesses do? And he held up his palms, don't even go there... and regaled me with tales of disobedient dancing sisters and magic shoes that could tango a girl to death.

He sighs and looks at Malik, then lets his eyes fall, just for a moment, on my stomach. He'll find no excuses there. Still flat and lifeless as a shield.

'Malik?'

'I'm sure I could procure one, your highness.'

'Have you heard any cases of any, er, loom trouble?'

'Not that I know of, your highness.'

'Well then, my love, of course you can.' He shines with pleasure and the affection in his eyes twists my heart and makes me long for the past.

He leaves me when it is still dark, and I run up to the tower to watch them all ride out. I stay leaning on the balustrade until the stars dissolve into the dawn and the birds start to sing – music to take the breath from your lungs. Already I miss him a little. The sky turns to pewter. It was a morning like this that I first saw him, riding out of a dawn mist. I heard the hoof beats first, and the jingle of the bit, and the snorting of his horse as he pulled it up. It was the broadness of his shoulders that struck me first, and then the kindness of his smile.

Malik brings me skeins of goat wool and a great clonking loom cut from green oak. Five men try to carry it up the staircase, up a bit, down a bit, to the left, to the right. They give up after an hour and throw a rope from the balcony and haul it up from the outside, their biceps ballooning and the ropes twisting and sighing against the wall. It takes me back to those early visits from the Prince; the weight of him on my dangling plait, my eyes puddling with the pain, my head visored between my hands, elbows braced against the stone balustrade. He was much heavier than the witch, but it was worth it for that first heart-jolting glimpse of his tanned hands gripping the wall. Then the pressure would lessen on my head, and he'd swing himself over, blocking out the sun and I'd wait for the warmth and hardness of his body as he took me in his arms. I used to think I was lightheaded from his touch, but now I wonder.

A woman comes with the loom. Twenty-four hours to teach me how to weave. Short and saggy, with arms and shoulders that look like she's borrowed them from someone else. There's something about her – her height and the line of her cheeks – that reminds me a little of my witch. Her fingers are quick and calloused, they twitch and fidget at her sides as she drops me a clumsy curtsy. I glimpse, for a wing-beat, the scorn in her face, and then it's gone. I'm determined to earn her respect. I ask her to call me Rapunzel, and insist she eats and drinks with me. She makes the warp first, bending into the machine, her hands falling into a rhythm, smooth as a dance, over, under, across. When she's done she takes it from its frame and lifts and chains and loops it onto the loom. *Tight enough to keep it safe, but not too tight to break it.* She points out the beater and harness and roller and raddles and spacers and sticks. She threads the heddles and sleys the reeds and ties knots and winds the bobbins. We haven't even started weaving. She constantly checks tension. 'Never too tight,' she mutters, 'it'll twist and snap and fly off.' When she says it's ready to start I watch her carefully and listen to her advice, but while her fingers dance and fly and twist, mine are slow and clumsy. At lunch time she fists meat and bread into her open mouth and chews like a dog. She swipes her face onto her shoulders – right, then left – while her hands are busy tearing at the wheat cakes and drumsticks. My witch had hands like that, greedy and grasping and strong. She used to brush my hair and massage my head. It was my only human contact – her fingertips squeezing and pecking at my scalp and the steady sweep of the bristles through my hair.

At dusk the loom-lady asks me if I'm tired. I shake my head and ring for Malik to bring more candles. The tips of my fingers are blistered and my neck and shoulders and back are burning. She doesn't return my smile, but the scorn has gone. She leans over to adjust the tension in one of the threads and for one miniscule wing-beat I think she's going to massage my shoulders. Witch would have done. I had to kill her to escape, everyone tells me I did the right thing.

'What's that?'

It's the first time she's spoken other than to deliver an instruction.

'A mirror.'

'You don't say.'

'It's a magic mirror. For the Prince and me to see each other.' Malik has positioned it on the mantlepiece, angled so the Prince can see the whole room. It doesn't reach the balcony though.

'How – *sweet*.'

We work through the night and at dawn she points to the paling sky and says she's done her time.

'Wait.' I lead her out to the balcony and show her what's in the chest in the corner under the corbel. 'Can I use this?'

She lifts her shoulders and stares out at the bloody fingers of cloud creeping up behind the forest. 'Unlikely.'

'But is it possible?'

'I've never used them. You can try. When you're more experienced.'

'Rapunzel!'

We both start.

'Rapunzel! Where are you? Who are you talking to? Rapunzel!'

The loom-lady cackles, wheezing and folding into herself like an emptied water skin. She shakes her head, sucks in air, and grabs my arm for balance. The dry whisper of her skin is the same as my witch's. 'Don't keep him waiting, Princess.'

The Prince watches as I bid her goodbye.

'Will you come again if I need you?'

She dips her chin.

'Rapunzel. You look worn out. Let me see you. Come over here. Nearer.'

I pick up the mirror. 'Where are you? At the port? Is that sea mist?'

'No my love, it's sunny.'

I realise it's just his breath fogging the glass. 'You're too close. I can hardly recognise you.'

'Undo your hair for me, Rapunzel.'

I take off the golden clip, tease out my plait and run my fingers through it.

'Now kiss me.'

The cold glass flattens and squashes my lips.

When I draw my face away the mirror is so steamed up I have lost him.

'When are you coming home?'

'Might be a while. There's a few boundary issues. Nothing to worry about, my love, just the usual rebels. Stay inside and you'll be safe. Don't worry, I'll be watching you.'

At night I sleep with the mirror on my pillow. The Prince likes me naked, my hair spread like a cloak across my skin. In the day he watches me from the mantlepiece while I sit and weave. I practise with goat's wool, then move on to the fluffsome slipperiness of llama. The Prince buys bales of it direct from the ships and sends it across to the castle. The cases smell of salt and foreign spices and have strange writing on the sides. Malik says they come from the Americas, where the rivers run with gold and the birds are all the colours of the rainbow and can talk.

'I'd like to go there one day,' I say.

Malik laughs and tells me the courier brings news that war has been declared between us and the Red Queen's kingdom. The Prince appears briefly in the mirror, says to stay in the tower where his men can guard me better.

When the llama wool comes back from the spinners I struggle with it at first. It is softer, smoother, lighter. Trickier to use, but it will be perfect for what I want. A month goes by and I weave each day, sitting by the open door, so I can lift my eyes from the threads and look out at the tree-tops and the birds freckling the sky. The loom-lady comes three times to redo my warp. She watches me weaving. I have found my rhythm, the ball of my foot pushing the treadle, my hands sliding from side to side to throw and catch the shuttle, slow and steady. She says nothing.

'Am I ready yet?' I gesture to the balcony. I have asked her the same thing twice before and she has shaken her head. Now she lifts her shoulders, and I am off my stool and skipping to the balcony and opening the chest. I bend down and grab handfuls of the stuff. Feathers. Thousands of them, collected over months and months. She shows me how to twist them into the llama wool. When I try they slip out, and when I force them in, the quills prick my fingers and they drift and float away, up and out of the door and over the balcony to dance and quiver in the briny air. Loom-lady barks a laugh and leaves me to it.

It is finished the day the Prince is due home. I don't know how to take it from the loom. It needs to be released slowly, carefully, so it doesn't unravel and disintegrate. I send for the loom-lady. She comes nodding and wheezing, reminding me more and more of my old witch. She hem-stitches the end with a bone needle, then twists and ties and unties and releases the ratchets and finally reaches into her pig-skin bag and takes out a huge pair of scissors. They trap the light and dazzle me for a moment, then the blades are scissoring the fabric and with one, two, three snips she cuts it free.

I wrap it around me; light and soft as air. 'It's a surprise for the Prince.'

She scratches at the wart on her chin, 'I bet.'

She helps me sew on woven straps. Close up, her hands looks as dry as the skin on the eagles' feet.

'Rapunzel! Rapunzel!' His face looms at me through the mist of his breath. I drop the cloak to the floor and pick up the mirror.

'I'll be home tonight.' His head cranes and his eyes search behind me. 'Who's that? Who've you got there?'

'Just the loom-lady.'

'Let me see her.'

She curtsies and leaves.

'Rapunzel. Let down your hair!'

I do as he bids.

'Leave it loose tonight. I'll be back at midnight.'

I feed the birds at dusk. They wheel and swoop and call to me in the fading light. I stand on tip-toe, flap my arms, and the cloak shifts and sighs against the air. I'm drawn to the mirror. Beside it, on the mantlepiece, are the scissors. They crouch there, empty of light now, dark as crows' wings. I lay the mirror on my pillow, take up the scissors, and with one fat snip slice off my plait. I fan it out, lay it like a curtain across the glass.

It's tricky climbing onto the balustrade. The Prince used to make it look easy. I try to imagine his face, but instead I see the witch, the shock and betrayal in her eyes as she died. I stand up, one leg, then the other, hold out my arms, let the cloak kiss the wind. I take a breath and let go.

MARISSA'S BIKE

There was something odd about Marissa coming to the beach that summer. She'd never liked the salt in the water that stitched rashy trails down her pasty legs, or the sand that gritted the snot on her upper lip, or the squash and the corned beef sandwiches Mum packed for us. She'd never really liked us, her cousins.

That summer she and I both turned fifteen. I had my six weeks planned out homework-less, Marissa-less, when she pitched up one afternoon with a brand new bike. Its wheels spun and a pedal grazed the paintwork of their shiny 4x4 as Uncle Ian dragged it out. I'd only seen Marissa at Christmas but she'd grown a foot and when she fingered her hair behind her ears, two tiny diamonds glittered in her lobes. Up in my bedroom she placed the blue Tiffany box in the middle of my dressing table and said I could borrow them if I ever got my ears pierced.

Uncle Ian and Auntie Karen were off to the Bahamas. Em, my kid sister, asked Marissa why she wasn't going and she just shrugged and said she didn't like sailing much.

'Are you still scared of crabs?' Em was hopping on one foot, one hand gripping her ankle, the other stretched out sideways for balance. She made it sound casual but I could see her expression.

Marissa shrugged. 'We don't get them in Surrey, unless they're cooked. Dressed crab, I like that.'

It was a good answer; it made me look at her carefully. Perhaps she'd changed on the inside too. Then she ruined it.

'And it's not just that I'm not keen on sailing, I think parents need time alone sometimes. We can be selfish can't we?'

Rich coming from her, the personification of single-child-selfish-syndrome.

'Are you coming to the beach tomorrow?'

'Guess so.'

'The fair's here.' Em released her leg and looked sideways at Marissa.

'I know, I saw it when we drove up.'

That was the one thing Marissa did like about visiting us. Her parents didn't approve of the fairground. But Marissa loved the rides, and she always had a pocketful of cash. On rare occasions she'd treat me, but normally we'd have argued by then and she'd go on alone, spinning round and round on the walzer or the twister or the octopus, her hair flagging out behind her and her face a pale smudge.

'We're going tomorrow night.'

'Cool.' And her sour-lemon face twisted into a genuine smile.

I had to sleep on the put-you-up and Marissa got my bed. I suggested Marissa could have Em's room and Em could sleep in with me, but Mum said I ought to share with Marissa in case she wanted to 'talk.' Rather ironic given that I wasn't allowed to bring up the one subject you'd think she'd want to talk about. Her parents were in the aftermath of another miscarriage. Mum told me as she was hospital-cornering my bed. We had to do sheets and blankets because Marissa was allergic to the feathers in the duvet. That made five miscarriages in total, and a baby that only lasted a week. Something to do with undeveloped lungs. That was ten years ago and that's why Marissa was so spoilt.

'Be nice.' Mum said.

Brighton summers are generally shite, but that year was abnormal. You slept with the windows open and woke up every morning knowing it was going to be another scorcher. You left the same pair of shorts on the floor and just stepped back into them. And no bras or pants, just a bikini underneath, so even if you were at home you could whip off your top and fling yourself on a blanket on the grass and tan.

I was tempted to make corned beef sandwiches to irritate her, but Mum had got some brie in and some nice rolls instead of the sliced stuff we normally had. She'd even bought some cans of coke and a punnet of grapes to take down.

In the garage Marissa asked whether I wanted to have a go on her 'Raleigh'. And I was so glad she said that, so I could blame my prickly irritation on her pretentiousness rather than her pierced ears and her legs and tits and the Topshop cut-away shorts she was wearing. I was nearly sixteen but when Marissa wheeled her bike out of the garage I stood behind her screwing up my face and mouthing 'Raleigh. Raleigh. Raleigh'.

'No thanks,' I said.

It was a weekday, and Mum and Dad were at work but it felt as sleepy as Sunday as we cycled down to the beach. A ginger tom dozed on the pavement and an old bare-chested man sponged his car in lazy, suddy circles. Em and I had cranky, gear-less bikes but it was all downhill and in any case, Marissa didn't remember the way, so she had to let us lead. We crossed over the A27 and down towards the docks and the beach, past the factory yards, their high, honey-comb wire fences sagging and coppered with rust. When we got to the locks the gates were up and we had to wait. Em and I made a show of chucking our bikes on the concrete and abandoning them to lean on the railings and watch the boats go by. A couple of trawlers chugged past, chunky and stained, the fishermen standing motionless, staring impassively ahead. Behind them came the flurried activity of a family sailboat. A boy about my age was hand-to-handing a rope. He squinted up at me for a second as he shook the hair out of his eyes. A girl who looked like his sister stood in the prow shouting words I couldn't understand. Their parents, tanned and casual, offered low-voiced advice. The whole family was kitted out in deck shoes and shorts. Suddenly the boy grinned and raised a hand in salute, and there was Marissa, next to me, leaning on her Raleigh, smiling and waving back at him.

'Dufour 40. Very cute. We had one of those for a while.'

I rolled my eyes at Em.

My lot were already on the beach. The usual spot, near enough to the cafe so it wasn't too far to walk, but as far away as possible from the shadow of the power station with its massive chimneys belching out their grey fug. On cloudy days it was impossible to tell where the smoke ended and the cloud began, but today the vapour was the only bruise on a bright hyacinth sky. Down on the beach the guys were straddling the grey-green horizontals of the groyne, all in board shorts, all smoking, their heads bowed and their cigarettes cupped between thumb and middle finger.

'Look.' Em was pointing at a boy cycling towards us from the dark rectangle of the power station.

'Who's that?' Marissa gathered up her hair and let it fall in a blond mass over one shoulder.

'Scott.'

My stomach constricted as he came closer. He was upright on the saddle, shoulders loose, one arm hanging with slack precision at his side, the other hooked around the curve of his surfboard. He was chewing gum, and the rhythmic movement of his jaws seemed to echo the steady rotation of his legs. He came to a halt in front of us.

'Alright?'

'Yeah. All good.'

'Nice bike.'

'Thanks. I'm Marissa. The cousin.'

She held out her hand and I started smirking but then Scott lowered his board to the ground and stretched out to take her hand in his. 'Hi Marissa, Sally's cousin.'

We left our bikes on the edge of the path and jumped the couple of feet down to the beach. I could feel Marissa hesitating behind me, she didn't want to leave her precious Raleigh up there, but she didn't want to make a fuss.

'Don't want to get this nicked.' Scott picked it up and lowered it down to the pebbles and she was wiping her hands on her denim buttocks and smiling and blushing a thank you at him.

We laid out our towels next to the others. Mine was some old stripy thing, thin and faded, and of course Marissa's was a massive fluffy Chanel rectangle. I plonked myself down while she neatened the edges and palmed out the bigger pebbles. She took off her clothes with slow, deliberate movements, blocking out my sun as she folded up her halter-neck and tiny Topshop shorts and adjusted the sides of her bikini bottoms. She turned to face Scott as she gathered her hair up with both hands and tied it back with a scrunchy slipped neatly off her tiny wrist. Out of the corner of my eyes I could see everyone watching her, the boys and the girls. She was all buffed and tanned and slim and curvy and she was wearing the white crocheted bikini I'd seen in town the week before. I couldn't buy it now.

'Nice bikini.'

'I like your nail polish. It's Rimmel isn't it? That the two-tone one?'

I closed my eyes and shut her out. The sun was still scorched on my retina and the bright circle shrank and shifted against my lids, sliding away each time I tried to catch it. Their voices gradually slurred to background noise and everything was reduced to sensation – the patchy pile of the towel against my palms, the heat of the pebbles against my heels, the scent of seaweed and sun-lotion and cigarettes, and then a waft of sulphurous egg and meat as somewhere nearby someone was eating a Scotch egg. The sounds were intensified, ebbing and flowing like the tide, carried across the water and over the pebbles, muted squeals as cold fluid touched warm flesh, snatches of conversation, the shifting crunch of stones as Marissa adjusted her position, the murmuring of the boys, the shuffle of paperback pages, the tinny base of headphones…

When I woke up only Em was there.

'Where is everybody?' I palmed a dribble of saliva from the side of my mouth.

'They made me stay to watch their stuff.'

'Where are they?'

'Claire and Sue are getting ice-creams, the boys have gone to buy more fags and Scott's teaching Marissa to surf.'

'There isn't any surf. It's as flat as a frigging board.'

'Don't worry, I told her you fancied him.'

'Jesus Em.'

Claire bought me a Magnum and the boys came back with packs of Camels and we watched Scott and Marissa walk up the beach together. Scott with his sticky, surfy hair and Marissa all flat-stomached and jutting hipbones. You could see she liked him. She was nodding and laughing, her hands painting the air as she spoke.

Scott sat on the edge of her towel, his feet on mine. I could see the salt gilding the hairs on his arms and legs. His mouth would taste of salt too, and his tongue. I know because he kissed me last week, and afterwards, when he whispered my name I could taste the briny vapour on his breath. Simon chucked him the Camels and he lit up, and when he pulled the cigarette away it stuck to his lower lip for a second like it didn't want to let go.

'So you coming to the fair with us tonight, Marissa?' He had his knees tucked up and he leant back as he exhaled and I imagined the warm weight of his torso resting against her legs.

'The fair?' She sat up and busied herself with unpacking the sandwiches.

My chest tightened.

Marissa laughed. That high, girlie tinkle, like water filling a jug.

'Not my thing,' she glanced sideways at me, 'Ask Em and Sally. I'm crap at all this stuff. The salt makes me rashy, the sand makes me itch and the rides make me sick.'

When we left I asked if I could have a go on Marissa's bike after all. The tarty gears were okay, but they didn't really make the journey much easier. So we cycled home at the same pace, three abreast, the sun behind us and the salt-spiked wind in our hair.

MATADOR

You'd be the first to say it's not right. You nod and touch it with the prongs of your fork. Right-handed. It's pasta, so that's fine. Spoon in left; fork in right. The spoon being the depository for the al-dente coils that you swizzle, soft and pliant, around the tines of your fork.

You'd be the first to say that this is wrong – this cool, coagulated gloopiness. Although there's the tiniest, teeniest little voice extolling the benefits of its pliability. It stays in your skull. You trap it. Mouth clamped shut lest it squiggle out. The voice says it's more biddable this way – cool and sticky. It'll fold itself around the fork without any surprising slippery trickiness. You ram the lid on the squeaking in your head. Den is right. You could not call this al-dente, and you would be the first to agree to the pasta's inedibility.

The sauce is another matter. These things improve with time. Sometimes. Not vongole. But this is just bolognese. Not just bolognese, of course. You have used Den's paternal grandmother's recipe. You concur that this can only benefit from a reheat. You have made the passata from home-grown tomatoes and home-grown garlic. The onions had to be bought. It was a damp winter, and despite the careful husbandry of your garden the stemphylium blight was your enemy. So not your fault. At all. Den acquiesces. He is aware, and forgiving of, the arbitrary forces of nature. The bacon is from the farm on Cranhurst Lane – organic, free range and fed on pine nuts. You're not sure you believe this. You've made a pine nut sauce; you know the cost. You don't argue though. You nod as the man wraps up the cold striated chunks at the farm-shop counter. There doesn't seem a reason to refuse to visit the farmer's pigs, so you nod and thank him. There is something pleasant about them. Their genial mud-larking, the curious snuffling, the perky complexity of their tails, their communal butting and nudging, and their pleasing markings that remind you of the plastic farm animals you had as a child. Yet you cannot forget Orwell. It is in the pale lashed eyes, and in the grunting that has a ring of certainty, of nuance. When the owner gives an encouraging flick of his chin, you pat them. You scratch the pleasant warmth of their bristly hides, and agree they look happy enough. You even feel a frisson of excitement at the passive danger. After all, what could they do to you?

Den nudges the plate with the heel of his hand. A centimetre or two. No more. Perhaps an inch. 'What d'you think?' he asks.

You agree. Best to start from scratch.

'If it's not too much trouble?' he says.

'No no.'

After all, you enjoy making pasta. If you go back to work you would like to market food this time. One day, when Carl is older perhaps. You'll broach the subject again in a couple of years. In the meantime you save up your words, letting them gather and simmer. Den has taught you his favourite recipes. He has translated his paternal grandmother's notebooks into a printed, bound file. Times New Roman, 12 Font, laminated for practicality. It is a time consuming and arduous task; his command of the language is limited and Google-Translate is not all it promises. Sometimes, when Den is at work, you look at his paternal grandmother's original notes: the faded ink, the extravagance of the tails on her fs and gs, the sauce spillages (that you suspect were remedied with a moist finger swipe), the oil-fattened paper, the flattened sprig of rosemary and the distant tang of garlic.

The farmer said something odd to you. Don't feel sorry for them. They've got it made. I feed them, clean them, talk to them. Life of frigging luxury. He leans on the fence, his waxed sleeve brushing against your jumper. If Den could see you now he would mutate into a farm animal himself. Metaphorically, of course. He is not a violent man, but he is very protective and there is something bovine in his anger, the way he corners you with words sometimes, and the bullish persistence and the thrust of his sharpened syntax. And of course there are his eyes. They had you that first day, with their beautiful, bovine liquidity, and the extravagant lashes. Love at first sight. You both agreed. Don't forget that. Don't forget that. But there is something porcine too. A cunning that leaves you as confused and tangled as these little beasties' tails.

You're not sure what to do with the fettuccine. It really is congealed now – solid and cold. Your choices are: a) the bin, b) the bird table, c) save it and eat it yourself tomorrow for lunch when Den's at work. Which one will be right today? All three have been correct on different occasions. You gather the plates and scrape the fleshy mass into a Tupperware coffin. You'll work out its fate later. It is just the two plates today; Carl is on a geography trip in Dorset. It is surely the wrong time of year for gathering topographical data on a windy peninsular, and he is a thin child. You packed him extra layers but there is no guarantee he will wear them. There is a tender gnawing in the pit of your stomach when you think of your son. He spends most of his time in his room these days, but you still miss the sense of him in the house. His brittle awkwardness, like dried spaghetti. It is perhaps just as well he is not here today.

You put the water on to heat again. In the pan. Den can taste the difference if you use kettle-boiled water. You scatter in a generous palm of sea salt. Den is a proponent of the adage 'as salty as the sea.' You have heard Nigella use that phrase but you don't tell Den as he is not a fan. 'As salty as tears' is the idiom that pops into your mind. When you were courting you cried once at the cinema. It was some silly, sentimental film. Den thumbed away your tears and kissed your face. His breath was tangy with garlic, his lips as soft and warm as penne.

A puffed sigh and a rustle prompt you to switch on the lights to facilitate Den's reading of the Saturday paper. The illuminated room jumps into the kitchen window. You are both there, in coupled otherness. Your doppelganger walks companionably to the freezer with you. You wouldn't have minded making the fettuccine from scratch again. You like the ritual, the certainty of the measurements and outcome. Den bought you a Marcato pasta machine for your last birthday. It is a marvel, you agree. A traditional, hand powered device, but with all the advantages of modern technology. It has nine thickness settings – from 0.33mm to 2.55mm – and the shiny, chrome-plated rollers guarantee no sticking. It is not fool-proof though. You must still exercise vigilance. Cleaning is key, and you never forget to dust it with flour and run a sheet of paper through the rollers before use. But you love the whole alchemic process. You are still in awe at the transformation of the dough beneath the steady rotation of the handle. You imagine generations of Italian women sweeping back in an endless, aproned line, kneading and stretching and rolling and cutting – hundreds of reflected doppelgangers. You wonder, sometimes, whether the paternal grandmother would have employed the same exactitude, but your precise methodology offers the reassurance of a guaranteed outcome. You are scrupulous with the ingredients and weights. You cool your hands in iced water, use 00 flour, 10% semolina, size 2 organic eggs. Nothing is left to chance.

There is a grunt and a foot-scrape from the kitchen table as you open the freezer. A well-respected cousin of Den's condones the practice of freezing fresh pasta, so Den is loathe to criticise the process, yet at an instinctive level he does not like it. Drying, not freezing is the historical method of preservation. The cold air spikes a thought of Carl. You forgot to pack his gloves. When you look at the drawer of labelled containers there is a gloopy surge in your stomach. Spaghetti (*little springs*), Capellini (*thin hair*), vermicelli (*little worms*), linguine (*little tongues*), lasagna (*cooking pot*), Fedelini (*little faithful ones*), but no fettuccine (*little slices*). Your gut gives another glutinous heave. Hunkered down on the floor there is not even the reassurance of your reflection. You wish Carl was here. His favourite is Fedelini. He does not like you and Den arguing, but on occasions his presence diffuses the situation.

The farmer, perhaps encouraged by your petting of the pigs, insisted on showing you the provenance of the minced beef. This is what caused you to forget the eggs. You are totally out. You would be more than happy to make another batch of fettuccine, but you cannot. You keep your head lowered, feel for the barometer of Den's mood over the hum of the fridge and the pumping of your heart. Your hands nest in the pocket of your apron. You work at the grains of semolina trapped in the seams. It is the paternal grandmother's apron. The red fabric is soft and thin with age. The week after your honeymoon, Den had tied it around your waist, circled you from behind, and huffed a kiss into the tingling skin of your hairline.

At the farm the bull was tethered to the fence. It stood solid and still on its weight-buried hooves. Gentle as a baby today, the farmer said. Go ahead, go ahead, it's safe to stroke him. Its hide rippled in response to your touch. You inhaled its musky, meaty heat, and when you offered your hand to the massive bulk of its head, its leathery nose, wet as a tongue, buried itself into your palm. The skin on its muzzle, beneath the tips of your fingers, was as delicate as the inside of your wrist. He reminds you of the bulls you saw with Den in Naples on your honeymoon. They used to hold bull fights there in Roman times, Den told you, up on your balcony on the *Piazza Mercato*. He fed you truffle bruschetta and pointed to the square below, whispering about the *Tauromachia* and kissing away the juice from your lips. There were newspaper cuttings in the hotel foyer, and a painting next to the bed of the *Tauromachia* revival in the 1800s. You lay spooned with Den, beneath the thin cotton sheet, staring at the picture while he slept. The bulls were smaller and slighter than this one at your local Surrey farm. It was the matador that pulled you in though. In the painting he is not flamboyant; he looks tired and scared. He is standing, tense and motionless, in his dusty, sweat-stained costume, the red cloth suspended from one hand, the other held out as if he is preparing to embrace the bull, or perhaps to marshal it towards him. His face is tight with concentration.

The linguine is the closest match. You shut the freezer, smooth your apron, and meet your reflection at the sink.

'Linguine okay?' You hold up the tub of brittle ribbons, your voice as light as air, a gone-already feeling in your groin.

'Don't worry. No hurry. Make some fresh. I can wait.' His voice is as light as zabaglione.

You grip the wedge of parmesan. 'I can't. There are no eggs.' You would be the first to say you have no real excuse. At the farm shop there were layered trays of them behind the till. White as skulls. Lined up like the rows of headstones at the Sangro Cemetary, where Den's paternal grandfather is buried. Where you stood together in the dusty heat, cradling him as he sobbed into your shoulder. You would be the first to agree it's not much to ask when he's up at the crack, working his fucking balls off, day after fucking day. You pare off slivers of cheese. Den likes parmesan. Behind you the chair scrapes. There is a shift in the air.

You look up at the glass and see your reflections. They multiply into an endless fedelini-ing line of couples. The aproned woman, the bull coming at her from behind – head lowered, flanks heaving, grunting. The first woman fusillis around. Her scarlet apron flares. She steps to the side. The horns – curved and extravagant and bone white – are a capellini-breadth from her face. She stares into the liquid, bovine eyes, and raises the frozen block of tagliatelle.

You open your eyes and let the tagliatelle drop into the sink. You can see the faintest imprint of your fingertips, where the warmth of your skin has started to melt the ice.

'Carl's away for the night.' You untie your apron and turn and smile at Den. He is standing a couple of feet away from you. You dangle the apron from one hand and let it drop to the floor. You hold out your arms and he comes to you, soft and pliant and al-dente.

Suicide Bomber

Tuesday morning and I've got a bomb in my pocket.

'Hurry up, Jen.'

I close the fridge door so slowly I can feel the magnet suck it shut.

'Jen.' Mum stabs her piping bag towards the clock, launches it at the sink and elbows on the taps. I slip my hands from the fridge to the thing in the pouch of my jacket pocket and curl my fingers around its fat fragility.

'I'm not leaving without you.'

She's been up since five, making about a hundred cupcakes for some toddler's party. They're all over the house, in varying shades of 'girl' – pinks and pastels, lilacs and lemons, all swirled and sparkled and scented. She started baking about a year after Dad died. Every spare second she had, trying to exorcise his ghost with rose water and vanilla essence, banish his memories in a puff of flour, icing sugar and glitter.

She sighs and wrings her hands in a Union Jack tea-towel. 'Come on, Jen, we can walk down together.'

'Should have worn sandals.' She glances sideways at me as we stride along, 'Jesus, Jenny, you're wearing a jacket. You'll roast alive.'

It's been the hottest July for a decade, but they said on the news last night it's going to break. You can feel the change in the air, the thick soupiness of it clogs up your throat when you breathe in. Along our street the leaves are hanging from the plane trees like they've given up, and the grass verges are as dry and brown as old tobacco. The beat of my heart is loud in my ears, tick, tick, tick, tick.

We stop at the corner. Mum looks at me and I keep my hand in my pocket and stab my feet at the dust.

'See you tonight then.'

This is where our journey splits – she heads for the tube, I walk to school. When I was in year seven we used to hug here, a big rocking ten second clinch. We'd count down: Ten, nine, eight, seven... Now I'm too old. She hoists up her bag again, 'Look, Jen, I was going to stay over at Mike's tonight, after I've delivered the cakes. You okay getting yourself supper?'

'Sure.' It's good that she's found someone else. That she's 'moving on.' I don't like him much, he's kind of creepy, in an earnest Louis Walsh way. All smarmy and do-goody and glass-half-full. Talks to me like he's my mate. Tells me Mum's 'on a journey.' That the baking's therapeutic. That the act of giving is healing.

'You still come first you know...'

'Mum. It's cool.' And I mean it. She needs someone now.

'How about you? You're not seeing Nat tonight, then?'

'No.'

My school's at the bottom of Kingstone Lane. It's a Roman road, so you can see the building from half a mile away, a pig-ugly 1960s' thing. Our sixth form's in the high rise bit, supposedly reflecting our status – top of the school. Some tarty designer put in these huge windows all round, not considering the cleaning budget and health and safety. Now they're splattered with pigeon shit and have been bolted down to prevent 'accidents.' I make myself walk faster, left, right, left, right, a soldier going into battle. A gladiator. Eyes forward, ignore the stuff flopping and churning in my stomach, keep my hands away from the thing in my jacket pocket. Past the trio of pine trees on the corner with their scattering of cones. Concentrate on the square of concrete looming up against the murky sky. This time yesterday it was bright blue, there were vapour-trail kisses high up in the ether, and I was still going out with Nat. Now the sky's bruised a grubby yellow-grey, and you can smell the sulphur in the air. The weather people have got it right for once, there's a storm on the way.

I swing my arms harder and clench my teeth to stop them chattering. If it wasn't for Mrs Stevens I'd still be going out with Nat. I read some posh magazine at the dentist once. It had a list of the most eligible bachelors, with a glossy headshot and a paragraph of their assets – financial and personal. If you did our school, Nat Taylor would be number one. He's got the looks, he's in the 'A' team for footie, his Dad's a builder, so he's loaded, and he's as cool as you like. I've fancied him forever. He asked me out three weeks ago. I was in *The King's Head* with Lynn, sitting at one of those picnic benches. Nat pitched up with a couple of his mates. He stood so close to me I could see the little crosses in the fabric of his shirt. I imagined shifting my cheek sideways, laying my skin against the soft cotton. For a second I was terrified I might actually do it, and I wanted to stand up and create some space, but there's no way you can get out of those seats and look cool, not in a skirt. So I sat there trapped, staring up at him, while he stood there looking like something out of the Vampire Diaries with his black hair and white skin.

'Cigarette?'

I shook my head. His ciggie was cupped between his thumb and middle finger, and when he exhaled he squinted his eyes and smiled at me through the smoke. There was this glow deep in my stomach, like someone had lit a fuse.

'D'you wanna come to Mambo's tomorrow?'

70

'Okay.'

And that was it, we were officially going out.

But not anymore.

Mrs Stevens is our English teacher. She came back last week after some mystery illness. I've always kind of liked her. She used to spend ages banging on about some random author or poet, but we didn't mind, somehow her passion sucked you in. I mean enthusiasm can be a real turn off, but with her it was contagious. She even managed to sell us Shakespeare. Daz and Scott Walker actually started laughing about Falstaff, I mean they weren't taking the piss, they actually found him funny. And she even got Phippsy into it, who's been off his head since his brother went to Afghanistan. She made it seem real, like it was stuff that could happen today; love and hate, politics and war. My very first essay, she gave me an 'A'. It was about Hamlet's faffing. I sneaked out a couple of plays from the library and took them home. I liked the way he tackled the dead dads, but it's the rhythm that creeps up on you. It got into my head, I started talking to Mum in iambic pentameters, even walking down the stairs in the same pattern, one leg then the other, der-dum, der-dum, der-dum, der-dum, der-dum.

But when Mrs Stevens came back last week she'd changed. 'Just write a poem,' she said. No pleasantries. Just get on and write. A 'free-writing session,' she called it. Suzie Crawford, the class swot, stuck up her mit, her fat face all shiny with certainty, and asked what the 'theme' was. Mrs Stevens shook her head, 'No theme, write anything you like.'

It was a mistake, you need to give the idiots in our class something to focus on, everyone was arsing about, texting each other, and flicking spit-balls, and when she finally cleared her throat and asked us to 'share our poems,' there were no takers. No thanks, Mrs Stevens, I've not finished, Mrs Stevens, mine's no good, Mrs Stevens. Every now and again her eyes would flick to me.

'David Turner, detention!'

'What've I done?'

She banged her palm on the table, 'Full detention. After school on Friday.' Her voice was all high and screechy and you could see this pink rash climbing up her throat.

Lynn leaned in towards me, 'She's gone loopy. Everyone's talking about it, she's given out eight detentions in one day, but they can't sack her cos she'll pull out the sick card.' Lynn stuffed her mouth against my hair, her breath all hot and huffy in my ear. 'She's had a mastectomy.'

'Shit.'

'You can hardly sack someone with one tit.' Lynn looked hopeful for a second, 'Maybe they'll have a full-out strike. No school for a week.'

When I looked at her again she seemed smaller and sort of lop-sided. She was wearing a loose cardigan, thin knit, with little pearly buttons down the centre that caught the light when she shifted in her chair. You could only glimpse the odd one because she had her elbows on the desk, and her hands clasped together under her chin. She used to be so cool, so in control. She'd never raise her voice, but she'd wrap us up in words. 'Words can be weapons, use them wisely,' she used to say. She made us highlight it in our copies of Hamlet: *Rapiers are afraid of goosequills.*

I jogged Lynn's arm. 'I'm going to read mine out.'

Lynn drew her finger across her throat, 'Social suicide.'

'Ben, would you like to share yours?'

'No thanks.'

'Susan.'

'It's not finished.'

Lynn shoved her exercise book towards me. She'd drawn a pair of massive tits in the margin. I shunted it back. 'I'm going to read mine out.'

'Don't.' Lynn giggled, 'You'll make a right *booby* of yourself.' She cupped her own tits with both hands.

'Would you like to share it with us, girls?'

We shook our heads but Lynn was still shaking with laughter.

'Full detention, both of you, tomorrow night.'

'But Mrs Stevens, I can't, it's Friday, I'm going out.' Nat was taking me up to London. Straight from school. His brother had an interview and the three of us were going up in his car.

'You should have thought of that, Jenny, before you started mucking about. Full detention, tomorrow. I'll see you at four.'

Then the bell went.

I don't see red. I've never understood that saying. For me it's like a giant hand is squeezing my guts. It's not all a bad feeling, there's a sense of liberation too, like you're so angry you don't give a toss about anything. I felt it then. The injustice. I was going to defend her. Save her. I used to have a reputation in my school for being hard. I used to lose my temper a lot. Dunno whether it's anything to do with Dad dying when I was six, maybe that's just an excuse. But I used to fly off the handle a lot. Anyway, a dead dad and a shitty temper earns you respect. If I'd read my poem out, and spoken to a few of the other kids, I'd have sorted it, I reckon. They'd have laid off her.

After the lesson she was on break duty with Mr Gibbs, the tech teacher. We'd told everybody about the mastectomy, and we were hanging out with half the class, sitting on the field in the sun, making daisy chains and sucking the sap out of grass stalks.

'D'you reckon they cut out the whole thing?'

'D'you think she's got it in a jar?'

'A pound of flesh?'

I waved a half-chewed stem at Mrs Stevens and Mr Gibbs, 'You reckon they're shagging?'

'You're joking.'

'Dead serious. Look at them.'

'Never. She's only got one tit.'

'Maybe she's asking him to make her another one.' I said.
Everyone laughed.
'Out of wood. A Wooden Tit.'
'No sagging. Nice and pert.'
'Varnished or stained?'
'It'll be stained soon!' It's Simon, he's a pig.

She was right. Words can be a weapon.

I started it off yesterday. After my detention. After Nat went up
to London with his brother without me, after he went clubbing in
the West End, and after he told me how cool the 'London Scene'
was. She was asking us if we had any questions about 'The
Merchant of Venice'. I raised my hand, slow as you like. Her face
lit up. 'Jenny, yes?'

She should have remembered her Hamlet, *Revenge has no bounds.*

'WOULDN'T IT be nicer if we went outside?'

'I'm sorry?'

I said it slower, with more emphasis, 'WOODEN TIT be nicer
if we went outside. You let us last year. WOODEN TIT be better?'

'A nice idea, Jenny, but I think it'll be cooler here in the
classroom. Now did you want to ask anything about Portia's
speech?'

'Mrs Stevens?'

'Yes, David?'

'WOODEN TIT be possible to look at act three again?'

'Well...'

'Mrs Stevens?'

'Yes, Scott?'

'WOODEN TIT...'

I could hear the whole class whispering it, *woodentit, woodentit,
woodentit.* The words spat and rattled like gunfire.

And her face went all strange, all still and flushed, and the heat
bled down from her cheeks to her neck, to the top of her blouse in

a big mottled stain. It was a loose, baggy blouse, with tiny birds and butterflies scattered all over it. Her hands flew to her collar and she held them there as if someone was going to rip it off. She was right about words. I felt a bit sick, my stomach swirling like the time I did cross country and threw up on my trainers.

Nat was waiting for me after school. He looked amazing, he must have skived off because he was in his jeans and T-shirt, and even though it was hot, he was wearing that leather jacket. And I was stuck in my crappy school uniform that I'd had on all day. He slipped his hand inside my waistband and tugged me towards him. When he kissed me, I could taste beer and cigarettes, and underneath it leather and sweat, and the spicy aftershave he wears. It was like I was inhaling him, layer by layer, and at the same time I was losing myself, dissolving on his tongue like one of those flying saucers Dad used to get me from the corner shop.

We went to the park again. I think I used to go there when I was small. I have this vague memory of being on the swing, an image of black shiny shoes paddling the sky, and Dad in front, with his arms out, waiting to catch me. But maybe I've just made it up. Sometimes I think I remember him, and then I find the picture in our album and I realise it's not a real memory, just a photograph.

Nat sat me on the roundabout and spun me round and round until I was dizzy. When I staggered off and pulled my hair away from my mouth, I could taste the metal on my skin, sour as blood. Nat laced his fingers through mine. He's got big hands – you can tell he's strong and sporty just by looking at those hands. There's a scar on his knuckles that glows white against his tan, when you kiss it you can feel the difference in texture, the scar tissue is all smooth against your tongue. He pulled me towards the bench and yanked me onto his lap.

'So what was London like?' I could see the Friday night girls, all skinny-hipped and skin-tight jeans, slinking and skanking on the dance floor. 'I wish I'd gone.'

'You should've come. Skipped detention.'

'I'll come next time.'

'Dunno if he's going again.' He put his hand on my lips, slipped his fingers into my mouth, then out and down, and under my blouse. He never talked much.

He unbuttoned my blouse, he was better at it than me, he did the whole lot one-handed – it's no mean feat, they're little buttons. And then he fiddled around behind my back and undid my bra and shunted it up, so it was sort of dangling under my neck in a weird lop-sided way. It made me think of a horse's nose bag. It didn't look very sexy. I didn't feel very sexy, and the whole dissolving thing had gone. He shoved up my skirt, and pushed me back on the bench. I couldn't stop thinking about my bag, which I'd dumped with my phone over by the see-saw, anyone could've nicked it. 'Nat. Wait a sec...'

He was all hot and huffy, and he was yanking at my knickers.

'Nat.'

'Shh... Come on, Jen.'

'Nat!' I got my hands on his shoulders and tried to push him off. 'Not here, Nat.'

'Jenny?' The voice came out of nowhere.

'Shit.' Nat levered himself off, fumbled with his flies, ran his hands through his hair.

It was Mrs Stevens, standing there, still and small, between the slide and the see-saw. 'Are you okay, Jenny?'

Nat put his arm over my shoulders. 'We're good. Come on, Jen.'

But my legs didn't work.

'Jen. You coming or not?'

'I...'

'For fuck's sake. I'll see you later then.'

And I still couldn't move. He left me there. He said something under his breath. Something horrible, I think. *Prick tease*, maybe.

But maybe I imagined it, because that's what I was kind of thinking. I watched him go, his jacket slung over his shoulder, his black hair glinting in the afternoon sun.

He dumped me that night on Facebook.

Mum brought me up a cup of tea, I could hear the shuffle of those silly slippers I bought her for Christmas, and the clinking of the spoon against the china. She knocked on the door. 'Fancy a cuppa, love.' She left it on the floor outside with a custard cream. Mum's not one for words. She says actions speak louder.

Now I'm marching into battle. A suicide bomber. The storm's driven the seagulls inland, and they're wheeling over the school, squabbling and mewing, and strutting fat-bellied on the roof. They're always bigger than you expect, there's one on the school gates, watching me with its lizard eyes as I walk through. I'm into the playground, into the school, the double entrance doors swishing softly shut behind me, down the science corridor, and up three flights of stairs to the English Department, tapping iambic pentameters on the thing in my pocket. It's in time with my heart. Der-dum, der-dum, der-dum, der-dum, der-dum. English is first period. I sit in my usual place, wait for the rest of the class to filter in, chairs scraping, bags unzipping, snatches of laughter, comments about *Big Brother* and *Facebook*. No one tries to speak to me. There's a lot of loud whispering and I think I hear the words *prick tease*.

I'm all alone, Lynn's not coming in today, she's got her driving test. I look around the room, at the posters on the wall. Hamlet and Yorick's skull, Ophelia floating peacefully amongst the reeds, King Lear clutching at his blind eyes, and some of the war poems we wrote last term. And then Mrs Stevens is here, clicking the door to behind her, face shuttered, scuttling to her desk, arms folded, cardigan wrapped around her. 'So, the Merchant of Venice.'

There's some sniggering, mutterings of a *pound of flesh*, and *wooden tit*, and I know they're ready to kill her.

I take a deep breath, shove my chair back and stand up. They all turn as I walk to the front. I'm looking straight ahead, but I can still see their faces, out of the corner of my eyes, like pale blurs, and I think of that poem we did by Ezra Pound, about people on the underground – *petals on a black wet bough*. My hand's trembling on the thing in my pocket, my heart's skittering and banging der-dum, der-dum, der-dum, der-dum.

'Jenny?'

Too late to change my mind now. I take it out of my pocket. 'This is for you.'

I peel away the paper and put it on her desk.

'Oh.' Her arms unfold and one hand reaches up to touch her mouth.

It sits there, pink and sparkly and sprinkled.

A cupcake.

'Thank you.' I say.

THE SINGING FISH

I bought the singing fish from a travelling salesman. A species I'd imagined as extinct as the rag and bone man. Mum used to tell me about them, when I was a little girl, how they'd come tapping at the door when she was my age, with miracle cures for the ailing housewife. He brought the things you didn't know you needed, she said. I imagined some strange hybrid, a Magic-Male-Avon-Lady, doffing his hat, with a white-toothed grin and cheap charm.

He came on a Friday morning. A normal Friday, Ed going to work, his goodbye-breath warm on my shoulder as I stood at the window. 'How bout seeing your mother this weekend?' He said, as he always does.

I stayed there after the door clicked shut, watching the darkness leach away and the houses opposite creep back into focus. You could tell it was going to be another scorcher. I closed my eyes, stretched myself out across the open frame, and imagined the flick of air against my face, perhaps the cool weight of a shadow, the tap of fingers, the scent of summer skin. But the air was soupy-still, and the only smell was the river. You can't see it from here, but you know it's there. They say it's hit a record low this year, the water turgid, the banks carved and cracked. Impossible to imagine its winter force, they say.

I watched the children in the street trailing past, in puffs of dust, shouting and shoving, skipping and yacking, with spiky fringes and plaits and red faces. Some saw me and waved, some looked away. The milkman came, with my two litres of semi, the granary and the bacon. I didn't see him though, or hear the knocker. It's a big old thing, I still polish it. It's Chloe's height, she used to laugh at her reflection, all fat faced and foreign. I look like a fish, she used to say, gupping her mouth up and down. I'd have heard it if he'd knocked, he usually does, or he calls through the letter box, a cooee, or a hello. Out of courtesy. I'm the perfect customer, I've tried everything in his little brochure. I must have been in the loo. I missed our chat, on the step. Any news? Then the usual litany of pleasantries. Hot enough for you? Who'd have thought it could have lasted this long? Small talk's underrated.

It was about ten-thirty when the figure appeared at the top of the street, a pencil sketch, scribbled on the skyline, gaining colour and definition as he came nearer. He was heading straight here. Past Vera and Barb and Mrs Coney at number 33. My heart was in my mouth, he approached with such purpose. He didn't glance down at the dried tobacco-grass verges, nor turn his head to take in the brazen colours in Sharon's garden, who keeps her plants alive despite the hosepipe ban. He must be a policeman, I thought, an inspector, perhaps in his dark suit. Then he stopped, and I could see the case he was carrying, and I started breathing again. No one official would deliver news with a box like that – some huge square, black thing, like my dad's old projector box, the one we used to watch the family slides on at Christmas. Or a magician's box. It made me think of the time Ed and I took Chloe to France, on *Brittany Ferries*, the overnighter. We let her stay up to see the magician. There were people without kids and Ed was laughing, in the way he used to, in silence, with his eyes watering, and his cheeks puffed out, and his chin dipping down towards his chest, as if he were embarrassed about letting it out. He kept asking what the heck they were doing there, without kids? We shook our heads and looked at our Chloe. She loved it – the tinsel and glitz, and the little shimmering frock his assistant wore. Until he made her disappear. She was only gone five minutes, but Chloe got all worked up. 'It's okay,' I said, 'she'll come back.' But she shoved herself off my lap, head swivelling, hands pleating the bottom of her dress. It was the blue and white striped one I got from the French catalogue, it's still in her wardrobe on the padded pink hanger Mum bought: *My Favourite Dress*. I thought she was going to howl, but then the woman burst out of some cupboard on the other side of the stage. Fanfare. New outfit. Good as new.

The salesman wasn't just stopping to re-adjust his grip on the box, or wipe the sweat from his face, he was talking to Mrs Coney's cat. I took the opportunity to stretch a bit, change position. I was kneeling on the seat Ed had made me, with the special squishy cushion, so my legs don't go to sleep. I shoved the heel of my palm against the sash and leaned out. He was bending down, holding out his hand towards the cat. It was a mistake, that cat's a vicious old tom. It had a crack at Chloe once, sent a ladder spinning up her tights. Not that she was fazed, she just came running home and grabbed a tin of *John West* out of the cupboard. She kept tuna in her bag for weeks, until she won him over. She was never the type to give up.

I was holding my breath, waiting to see what the cat was going to do. Perhaps it was that squat, black box, or the stillness of the morning, or the fug of sulphur in the air, that was turning the factory smoke a grubby yellow, like an old bruise that's getting better. Whatever the reason, my heart was juddering, and I was expecting something special. From here he looked like one of Chloe's Pelham puppets as he hunkered down, folding and concertinaering in on himself. He reached his hand out, slow and gentle, and then I saw the sudden spasm of his body as he snatched himself back, jerking away, his arms windmilling as he toppled over onto the pavement on his backside. It was as if some giant hand had slashed his strings. His yell reached me a nano second later.

I laughed, a strange huff of a sound that came up from my stomach to my throat, and the back of my hand was against my mouth, and I caught my reflection in the side window, and I looked like my mother.

I was still smiling when he knocked at the door. He stood there in his charcoal suit, a polite pace away from the threshold. 'Morning Maam.' Like an American cowboy.

'How's your hand?'

'You saw that?'

I nodded and, when he held out his hand, knuckles up, I took it in mine. It felt strange, that physical contact. It was a nice hand, tanned, flesh-levelled nails. Clean – he didn't work in the factory. There was a row of raised welts across his skin, oozing blood and fluid.

'Come inside. I'll get some cream.'

He followed me in and I caught him looking through the open door into the spare room, where my bed was still unmade from last night. I lead him into the kitchen, the first aid stuff is in an old shortbread tin under the sink. It caught me unawares for a second and I was glad my back was turned when I prised off the lid and looked inside.

'I've got all sorts here.' My voice was fine. 'Perhaps you should wash it first. The bathroom's just through there.' It's straight off the kitchen, the neighbours have had theirs moved. But I don't mind it, it was handy for toilet-training and Ed used to leave the door open when he came home from the factory. He'd tell me stuff about his day while he showered, his voice slipping out with the steam, as I stood at the stove making supper. We used to talk about having an en-suite put in, for Chloe. She'd already chosen the sign for the door, this kitsch silhouette of an old-fashioned tub bath, with a little girl, head and shoulders safely above the waterline.

I put the first aid box on the table in front of him. 'Antiseptic cream? Bites, stings and grazes. Or maybe *Calomine*.'

'You've got the lot.'

Calpol, Tellytubby plasters, teething gel, *Infacol.*

'*Piriton* – that's best. And it's still in date.' I gave him a proper spoon, the plastic one didn't seem right.

'This'll work, will it? Ease the sting?'

'Should do. Might take a while – it's nasty, you'll have scars.'

The lid was a bit gritty, where it hadn't been used for so long, but he got it open, and it was fine inside. He didn't say anything, just tipped it slowly into the well of the spoon. I looked away when he put it into his mouth.

'It should stop the pain.'

He was filling up the spoon again.

'Would you like a cup of tea?' I put the kettle on, dithered for a second, over the Willow Pattern or the mugs. I chose the Willow Pattern, Chloe liked the pictures – a scene frozen in time, lovers on a bridge, and swallows scissoring a china sky. It's a small kitchen, and I had to step over his box to get to the larder. 'What made you come here?' Close-up the box was even bigger.

'I sell stuff.'

'But why here? To this house? You came straight here.'

'Did I?'

'Yes. Sugar?'

'Just milk. Should I sit down?'

'Sure.'

He didn't move.

'Just sit...' And that's when I realised he knew. I saw his expression. He was afraid he'd sit in the wrong place. In Chloe's place.

'So why did you come?' I wasn't angry, most people know anyway. It's an old story now. He took the seat opposite the fridge. I could see him out of the corner of my eye as I filled the teapot. He was staring at the photos. The fridge door's plastered with them. All stuck on with a magnetic alphabet. It's partly how I taught Chloe to spell. As she got older we used to write messages to each other with them.

PE tomorrow
get marmite
packed lunch Fri
Luv u

'I see you at the window.'

'Oh.' I sat next to him and poured out the tea.

'This is a short cut for me. To the office.' He cradled his drink with his damaged hand. 'Well, garage really. With a desk. I sell stuff on Ebay.' He kept his eyes on the cup-people on the bridge. 'I do all hours. Early mornings. Late nights. Have you seen me? Red Fiat. With a taped wing mirror.'

'That's you, is it?'

'I just catch this glimpse, of your face, at the window. Always there. Whatever time I pass.'

He was just a boy really. Eighteen, nineteen. A few years older than Chloe.

He peered over the rim of the cup. 'I wanted to ask. I mean, it's been bugging me. Are you there, at night too?'

'Sometimes.' The city's beautiful then, sometimes you get the edge of the sunset, seeping across, bright as fire opal. Like the picture Chloe did at school, where you do a wash of colour, and then sketch on the skyline afterwards, with charcoal. Hers was vivid mango, and she put in the river, curving round the town like a black rope.

'You stay there all night?'

'I try and sleep, in the spare room, so I don't wake my husband.'

'One of your neighbours bid on something. Collection only. I asked about you.'

The picture's upstairs on her bedroom wall. The sky's faded to a dusky peach, and the river's grey now.

'She said it was a car accident.'

'On the bridge. No one's fault. Ice. Mum survived.'

'Your daughter?'

'They've not found her yet.'

'Do you blame your mother?'

'Not really.' I sipped my tea. 'I know it's not her fault, I do see her, but she thinks we should *try again, have another one*. She said *Another One*.'

His eyes slipped away from mine and he turned his gaze to the bridge on the cup and murmured, 'Heard melodies are sweet, but those unheard are sweeter.'

It was stupid of me to let him in. He could be a psychopath. Or one of those weirdos who tell me they can 'reach beyond the grave'.

'It's Keats.'

'Oh. The poet?' So he's one of those. You'd be surprised how many people do that when they know. Mostly it's prayers, or passages out of the bible. Occasionally a poem. Sometimes one of those corny little American books full of homilies. They used to drop them through the letterbox, or give them to Ed to pass on to me, as if my grief gave them some new authority. Not that I minded, there's nothing left to mind about. I wait for him to elaborate, to start chucking out wisdom.

'Keats – he's writing about the scene on an urn. How time is frozen in art, how it'll stay like that forever, even sweeter in your memory, I guess. He died young.'

'Not as young as Chloe, she left a year ago.'

'But you think she might still be alive? Might come home?' He shunted his chair back, bent down and unstrapped the leather bands on his box.

'She used to swim there in the summer. In the river.'

I'd wait with a towel, and she'd come out beaded with water, her hair in sopping rat-tails and her body cool and solid against mine. Her skin still smelling of her, beneath that brackish river smell.

85

'So you're always waiting?'

'Supposing she came back and I wasn't here? I know what you're thinking, what everyone thinks, but it's possible, she swam like a fish. She got badges. I sewed them onto her costume. So many, we ran out of space.'

He nodded, earnest, eyes serious. He was a nice boy, Chloe would have liked him.

'And in any case I don't like going out, people don't know what to say to me.'

He delved in his bag. 'I've got an idea. I've got something, I think...'

'You hear stories... People turning up years later, after they've lost their memory...'

He was rummaging inside, practically up to his armpits. Mary Poppins. I wondered what he had in there. Miracle cleaning agents, pretty ribbons, hair slides, perfume? For a second I wished my mum was here, not that she'd have wanted any of that stuff, she was a mother, her accessories were aprons and oven gloves, her perfume was TCP and chicken stew.

'How about this? I thought...' He pulled it out.

Fish have always looked prehistoric to me, gaping and sliding in the shadows, like they're searching for a past world.

'It's a talking fish. A bass.'

It was madness, yet for one moment I imagined this fish bringing me a message, from Chloe, telling me she was living beneath the sea, a mermaid, or stuck in the belly of Jonah's whale.

'It talks. It's got a sensor. With a message. Hang on a sec, I'll switch it on. Now wave your hands in front of it.'

It was a huge rubber thing, green and gold and strangely muscular. I shook my head 'I don't need that. Why would you think I'd want...?'

'Wait.' He put it on the table and moved his arms, like windscreen wipers, clearing away the rain. It leapt into motion, flicking its tale, turning its head, grinning inanely at me as it began to sing: *'Don't worry. Be happy.'*

'Mad, isn't it?' He was grinning too, and for a moment he looked like a fish himself with his wide mouth and his wet round eyes. I felt my anger slide away.

'Here.'

I let him place it in my hands.

'Chloe would have loved it.'

This morning I am all prepared. I put the fish in the alcove, by the door, on the telephone table. I adjust angles and heights, and finally it sits waiting in the shadows on top of the Yellow Pages. It is all ready to go – customised by my strange salesman, so I can put in my own tape, with my own personal message. I imagine Chloe watching as I test it out. I think she'd like it.

Ed comes home, slow-stepped and seamed with black. He triggers it off as he walks into the hall. It flaps its tale and opens its mouth,

'Hello Chloe, if it's you, then welcome home darling, I'm not here but...'

Ed flinches and stops. I see something swirl and flicker in his eyes, then he shutters his face and shuffles silently into the kitchen. I don't know what I expected. He locks the bathroom and showers for a long time. When he comes out he lowers himself into the chair opposite me and forks in his bacon and egg. 'This is nice, love.'

I watch him eat, he's thinner than he used to be, and he's growing a beard. Maybe a week's worth already, it's the first time I've noticed it.

Later I sit on the window seat and he sits in his arm chair, and we watch the news together. There seem to be people dying all over the world. At 10.30 he levers himself up, presses his lips to my hair. 'Good night.'

I follow him into the hall. The fish is waiting with its watery welcome, batteries charged, voice ready.

'I'm coming with you.'

He stops, his body still twisted in retreat, shoulders hunched.

I lay my palm against his cheek. 'Let's go to bed.'

His face folds up and his mouth opens, and he makes this noise that comes from somewhere deep in his stomach. When I hold him, I remember the shape of his body, and the way we used to fit together.

Silent As Storks

The bird looks at me with shiny button eyes. I stare right back, and then the shot pans out and I see the nest and the tangle of aerials and satellite dishes and the tiles covered in bird crap. I blink and take a breath. Everyone's been talking about them. Lost storks, from Europe. Half the town is UKIP and some Pole got stabbed in Whitehawk last week, but we're setting up a welcome party for a pair of European Storks. They've lost their flock. Munster, that's the proper name. Suddenly everyone's an ornithologist.

I grab the remote. 'Grace.'

She pokes a podgy finger at the screen. 'Look.'

One of the birds is trying to ram a strip of yellow plastic into the jumble of twigs and rubbish. Its long, gaviscon-pink beak jabs and pokes at the nest.

'I'm not waiting.' I stab the mute button.

'Two minutes, Fin. Hold still, Grace.' Gran's got her tongue between her teeth.

'Nearly there.' Her fingers stumble on the slippery satin as she ties off the first plait.

My phone vibrates again and I swallow back a swirl of nausea. 'We've got to go.'

'First time in six hundred years. Who'd have thought it.'

The stick tumbles silently down the tiles and the stork stretches out milky wings, paddles the air and launches itself off the roof. I turn off the TV.

'We're going to miss it.' I palm back the cuff of my hoody. There's no watch, just the ghost of the face and strap, pale and shiny as a scar.

'They're supposed to be good luck.'

I shove my fists into my pockets and try to ignore the clenching in my stomach.

'Done.' Gran tweaks the finished plait. 'We could do with a bit of good luck couldn't we, love?' She kisses the top of Grace's head. 'One for you, and an extra one for your mum. Make sure you give her my love.'

The bus stop's empty.

'Have we missed it?' Grace sucks on the ratty end of her plait.

'No.'

'When d'you think it'll come?

I shrug and stare up at the sky. There's a glimpse of movement, high above the rooftops, a flash of white and an impression of a clunky wing-beat, and then Grace is yanking at my arm and pulling me off balance. When I look again it's gone, the sky's just an empty expanse of paving-slab grey.

'What you looking at?' She's tugging at my sleeve, jigging up and down, her mouth a wide elongated 'O.'

I squat at her side and shove my face against hers. 'Shut up.'

'What is it? Was it the stork?'

'It's nothing.'

'I want to see, Mummy! Mummy!'

I clamp my hand over her mouth. 'SHHHH!' A microcosm of spit flicks out and fizzes against her cheek.

'Morning.'

The old woman's appeared out of nowhere. She stands squat and still with her tartan trolley bag and shapeless wool coat.

'Where are you two off to then?'

I wait for Grace to gabble an answer, but she's in the corner of the bus shelter, muttering to herself and ramming a patent toe into the shattered glass where someone's bricked the window.

'Bit late for school, aren't you?'

My phone vibrates again. I swallow and stare at the ground. The silence balloons out between us.

'D'you go to King's Manor?'

I close my eyes for a second, my head swirling. I'm back in the school bogs, with my head against the toilet bowl, and Darren Fisher's Doc Martin on my cheek and the sound of the flush and the sucking whirl of water.

'Our mum's ill. We're visiting her in hospital. Southlands.' I hold up my carrier bag with the box of Thorntons.

'Nothing serious I hope.'

'Bus should be here by now.' In the morning it's never late, there's no excuse to skive school; it comes farting and fizzing up dead on 8.20. Now there's no sign of it. Maybe I should abandon the whole plan.

'And to the green.' Grace tugs at my sleeve. 'You said we could go to the green didn't you Fin? To see your friends?'

'Do I know you?' The woman has edged closer. Her bag is nudging at my shins.

I step into the road, make a show of peering for the bus. 'We've just moved here. To live with our gran.'

'You're brother and sister? You don't look alike.'

We do look different. Grace is sort of low and squat and soft. I'm the opposite – all angles and edges. At my old school they used to call me 'stork.' Everyone had nicknames. I liked it, the familiarity of it. Alright then Stork. Some boy in art class drew me once. I liked that too – the thin scraggle of my legs and the lanky, cartoon sketchiness of my body. At this school it's different. Thin-ness makes you vulnerable, undefined. All the other boys are solid.

They're more the muscular 3D curves of a thick felt pen than my HB scrawled frame. Sometimes I dream that I disappear, that I'm erased in a single swipe of a white brick Staedtler.

'So d'you look like your Dad?'

I unknot my fists. Nosy bitch. But at least it's keeping Grace quiet. She's hopping from side to side now like she needs the loo, but she's shut up for once.

'Guess so.'

'Auntie Pat says he's buggered off.'

'Shut up Grace.' I shake my head at the old woman. 'He's working away, that's all.'

'What did you say your name was?'

'Here's the bus.'

It heaves round the corner, brakes grumbling, doors hissing and flapping open. I let the woman on first. She's all smiles. 'Thanks, ducky. Hello Mike, thought it'd be you today. Seen those storks yet? They're on your route aren't they? Had any twitchers? They'd get a good view from the top deck.' She's wrestling with her purse and the fat double ball catch, sticking out her tongue like Gran does, and shaking her head. 'They reckon they'll nest here for a while.' She starts fishing around in her pocket. 'Just the two of them. They're monogamous you know. Mate for life. There's a few people I know could learn from them.'

Whatever she's looking for must have fallen through to the seam of the coat. She's down to her elbow, her hand flapping about like something trapped. She makes me think of Darren and his gang. They slit the lining of their blazer pockets so if they're searched their flick-knives will slide slickly to lie in the hem of their jackets. I was going to do the same today. I even had the kitchen knife in my hand, and was imagining how it would feel, bumping against my thigh. Then Grace walked in. *I'll tell Mum.*

Now I'm weaponless.

'Bring your sister,' Darren said.

'Mute. Fancy that. Something wrong with their throats. Beaks as long as your arm and they can't make a sound.' The woman cackles. 'Know what you're thinking. Same as my Reg. Chance'd be a fine thing.' She clutches her purse to her chest, laughing until her breath runs out.

The bus driver manoeuvres back out into the road, hairy hands crossing as he pulls at the huge steering wheel. 'Come on mate. We're late already. Where you going?'

Grace is hanging onto my jeans. 'Are we going to see Mum?'

'Two halves to Southwick Square.'

'How old are you then?'

'Fifteen.'

'Bunking off?' The driver's eyes flick to my face.

'Dentist.'

'Yeah, right.' But he rings up the fares and hands me the tickets. The bus accelerates and we walk, wide-legged, down the aisle. Grace is in front, giggling and yacking, loose-kneed and chubby legged, arms spread out like she's flying. She passes the stairs to the top-deck and heads for the old woman.

'Grace, upstairs!' I wait with a hand on the rail. She normally likes it up there, peering into flat windows, squealing when I scratch my name on the seat or gob down at passers-by.

'Come on Grace!'

I'm about to go up when a pair of feet appears on the stairs. My heart wobbles. They're brown shoes with the toes slightly turned up so you can see the wear on the tip of the sole, where the rubber meets the leather. I hold my breath. They're polished on the top, and beneath the jeans you can see laces that look too new for the shoes. Like Dad's shoes. The legs thicken to thighs, the denim paler over the knees. A hand appears on the rail, a smoker's hand. Like Dad's; the fingers yellowed with nicotine.

'Excuse me.'

I step aside.

I turn to call Grace again, and now she's kneeling on the seat all cosy with the old woman. She's got a sweet in her hand, and she's chatting away as if she doesn't have a care in the world.

'Grace!' I'm up the aisle and I'm standing over them, the old lady and my stupid, smiling sister and my arm's whipping back and I'm slapping the sweet out of her hand, and her face distorts and her mouth yawns into a wail.

'She's not allowed to take sweets from strangers.' I grab her hand and drag her to a seat further up the bus. I sit by the window, rest my head against the glass, and watch the world fly past through my sweaty breath.

'Fin! We're here.'

The mass of the hospital blocks out the light. I bend forward and look across the aisle, and see, past the grubby bubblegum heart stuck to the pane, the two massive chimneys spewing their black stain across the sky. Darren said it was bodies. All the carcasses of the people they couldn't save, he said, piled up and rammed in and burnt away to nothing. There's a flash of white against the bruised sky, and I'm out of my seat and across the aisle, crouching to see better. But it's gone.

'Fin, we're here!'

The plan was to get off at the next stop, not here. I've got to get my watch back. We can see Mum afterwards. I need my watch. It was Dad's. *You have it, for luck. Keep it, til I get back.*

I touch my wrist. Darren's got it now. I tried to buy it back, but Darren just stuck his face into his Spar bag. His words came out through the crackling paper as it sucked softly in and out, If you want it back, bring your sister. Pointless trying to talk him out of it. Although I did. I tried.

You want yer watch back, just fucking bring her okay?

Grace has smoothed out the mint wrapper and is stroking the polar bear with a pudgy finger. She's forgotten the lost sweet already. Like she's forgotten Dad. Short-term memory. She'll be fine.

'Anyone for the hospital?'

Grace unpeels herself from the seat. When she stands up her skirt's rucked up so you can see half her arse, and she's left a sticky imprint of her bare thighs, all moist on the plastic seat.

'Let's see Mummy.' She's dragging at my wrist, hanging on with both hands, letting herself drop on the floor. A dead weight.

'Don't you want to meet my friends first?'

'I want to see Mummy.'

I could leave her at the hospital; could try and sort it with Darren. I've got some meth I could try and trade for it. Depends what mood Darren's in.

In the foyer Grace bounces towards the lifts. My head's pounding. A trolley click-clacks past on rattling casters. Nurses shout numbers at each other. Their white clogs clatter across the fake marble. The sheeted body is motionless and I catch a glimpse of glasses and the wet glint of a slack mouth. It makes me think of Mum. Upstairs on the fourth floor, with the wires and tubes and her face as grey as school-dinner-gristle. She's got a bed by the window. She's always looking out when we go and visit. 'Isn't it beautiful?' she says, and goes on about the autumn colours. When it's just trees rotting. I can smell it. Last time Mum tried to talk about Dad. 'Look Fin, I know how you feel, but don't hold out your hopes.'

I couldn't look at her, at her huge eyes and the bones pushing through her skin like they were trying to get out. She reached out to touch me, her hand scuttling across the bed like a spider. 'Don't worry. You're different from him. I can rely on you, can't I, love? You're doing a great job looking after Grace.'

I ram my hands in my pocket, feel the glue and the meth, know they won't be enough for Darren. 'We've got to go to the park first, Grace.'

Down by the sea the air's like soup. When we get to the green a group of blokes appear out of the mist. They've got binoculars and cameras and notebooks and they're yacking and smiling. They nod at us. 'You've missed them mate. Won't see a thing in this.'

Grace laces her fingers tighter into mine, and we push on into the damp fug of salt and seaweed and tar.

'Isn't this where the boys fight, Fin?'

'No.'

'Mum said it's not nice down here.'

I jerk my hand away and head for the old toilet block. They're all inside, Darren, Matt and Shaun, huddled over their paper bags. Darren has his sleeves rolled up. Dad's watch is strapped to his wrist. Grace seems fine. She's pleased to see them. She runs in, touches one of the urinals –

'What's this, Fin?' She twirls round so her skirt flares up and out. I can't take my eyes off her shoes, spinning, black and shiny amongst the used condoms, broken needles, and old newspapers.

'Hello lovey. Show us yer knickers then.'

I stare beyond her, through the broken pane, into the dying leaves of the oak tree at the corner of the playground. The silence is so complete I can hear the hissing whisper of the wind in the trees. There's a burst of laughter, the back-of-the-class-type-snigger. Grace is clutching and bunching the fabric of her tunic. Her pants say SUNDAY. Pale lilac, with puppies peering from outsize eyes through the letters. They're all still laughing, only it's different now – it's louder than in class; there's no teachers here.

There's a little line in the front of Grace's pants, a tiny vertical indentation, under the N on the Sunday, in the centre of the bit where the fabric dips in a gentle U between her pudgy thighs, like the imprint of a blunt knife in soft butter. They're all looking at it.

I can't stop staring at it myself, at the femaleness of it. It's not like it matters, she doesn't understand, sometimes she runs around the lounge stark-naked, or yanks up her nightie and dances along with the idiots on *Strictly Come Dancing*.

It's not like they're going to hurt her, Darren's a vicious git, but he's got limits. All he wants is a look, the sick wanker. And Grace is happy enough, glad to be the centre of attention for once, to be the focus of the big ones. There's no reason I should feel so odd, but I've got the same acidic wave pushing at the back of my throat as when I did cross-country. My stomach feels like the day Dad left, when he gave me the watch. Keep it safe son and I'll be back. Afterwards I spewed up alphabet spaghetti, and tried to make some sort of sense out of the mangled letters on my trainers.

Darren has put down the glue and is standing over Grace, pointing a finger at the letters on her pants. 'You've got the wrong day sweetheart. Today ain't Sunday.'

She giggles, bends her knees and drops her head to peer under her skirt. I stare at the skull-white slit of her parting. Her two plaits have fallen upside down and are dangling either side of her head. Darren reaches out, and I see the flash of Dad's watch as he gives each plait a tug.

Darren pulls harder on the thick blond ropes. 'Up-sa-daisy.'

'I gotta go mate.'

For a second I think I've said the words myself, that my thoughts have shoved their way out of my head. But it's Matt's voice and it's Matt who's turning to go. Matt who's got a sister himself and is up for a bit of shop-lifting, a bit of handbag grabbing when the rewards can be spent down the pub or the offie, but this isn't his style. Darren doesn't look up. 'Fuck off then.'

I can't tell whether it's the swearing, or the strange excitement in Darren's voice, but Grace's face has changed. Darren is still hunkered down next to her, but she's let her skirt drop and is chewing at a plait, twisting it round and round in her mouth.

'Let's take 'em off then. You can't go around with the wrong pants can you mate?'

She'll smile in a minute. Or giggle, the way she does when Mum blows raspberries on her stomach. Darren has no staying power, no attention span, ADS or something. He'll be bored in a minute. And Grace's got such a short-term memory. I'll buy her a sherbet dip from the newsagent, a whole bag of them, whatever she wants. She just needs to be quiet and then it'll be over and I can have Dad's watch back.

Grace makes a noise. A muffled explosive puff. It could be the start of a laugh, but her lower lip is fattening and trembling, and I know it's not. Her eyes are closed so tight I can only see the tips of her eyelashes, like a row of stitches. Please, Grace, please. There's nothing I can do, not against the two of them. The watch disappears as Darren's hands slip under Grace's skirt. It glints into view again as he tugs down the thin cotton of her pants. I can just make out the dials that show the times across the world: New York, Paris, Hong Kong. Somewhere across the planet Dad's out there. Grace looks at me, her face creased. 'Fin, I want to go home.'

I stare at my wrist. The scar of the lost watch is like the imprint of light on your retina when you close your eyes.

'Fin.'

There's a sudden clattering. A scraping and sliding and for a mad second my heart leaps. 'Dad?'

'It's the stork.'

We stare through the gap in the jagged corrugated iron. The bird is bigger than on the television. The massive, prehistoric beak is pinker and longer. It shivers and stretches and its wings unfold, smooth and layered and fat with feathers. 3D with them.

Shaun's up on his feet, laughing and pointing and fishing out his phone. 'It's the fucking lost bird. The Argus'll pay for a photo.'

A feather spins lazily through air.

Grace yanks up her pants, and runs to me.

Darren's fisting his forehead. The Spar bag hangs loosely from his other hand. 'What the fuck is it?'

The stork's strange reptile eyes stare right through me.

Grace tugs at my arm, opens her mouth, says nothing.

The black pupil dilates. I wonder what it's thinking. Whether it misses its family. Its head moves and the hole in the roof is filled with white. There's a glimpse of a skinny, elongated leg, and then it's gone.

'Fin?'

'Okay.' I take her hand and turn away.

'Oy, Fin. What about your watch?'

I shrug. 'Keep it.'

As we walk across the green the fog splits and dissolves. Grace tucks her arm through mine. I wait for her to say something, but for once she is silent.

'Look.' I say, and point up at the sky. The pair of them are way above us, their wings beating in time, slow and steady in the salty air.

The Deer

If I were to offer up an excuse, it would be the overhead mirror; our coupled otherness. The way the reflection reduced us. I don't tell this to Andy, three weeks afterwards in the fumy safety of the city. It's my favourite London pub, at the back of Tottenham Court Road. His choice, so while my heart is skittering, I am tentatively scenting victory. It is winter, the tail end of January, the time when the New Year celebrations are forgotten, but when the preceding year still haunts you in a hastily scribbled date on a form or cheque book. A time when your guard is lowered, and you realise you've rewritten the past.

Andy wants me to explain. When I order a coffee he puts his hand on my wrist. 'Don't you want wine?'

I shake my head, and so we have two cappuccinos.

'I'm glad you came.' His eyes are fixed on me. 'Kate? What happened? Where did you go?'

I shut out the flash of peeled skin, raw flesh, arched spine, and concentrate on my first impressions of Angmering. The briny shush of the sea on the pebbles, and the saline stench of the weed shoved up by the spring tides. The private estate Andy's father lives in is sandwiched between the coast and the South Downs. It is late December. We are newly engaged. Just back from Germany. Neither of us has met the other's family, although their geographical proximity is a coincidence that fuelled our courtship in Munich. We discovered we were both from Sussex, both considered ourselves Brightonians, had been to the same night clubs and restaurants. We spoke with the same southern rhythms, the same stretched vowels. Our bodies shared the same morphology. Colleagues commented on our similarities, our perfect pairing.

'Kate?' Andy breaks into my thoughts. 'Do you want to smoke?'

His thin shoulders are already hunched forward, his palms pressing the table.

'Okay.'

We met smoking. He handed me a faux-fur wrap – a signature of the slick Stüttgart bar we were in – a courtesy to protect you from the elements. There were fire pits and shawls and cow hides in the winter, straw hats and parasols in the summer. Andy was a graphic designer, arty, slight, cultured. Not my usual 'type'. We exchanged pleasantries and discovered our shared history. At the time there seemed something almost prescient in the thread of coincidences that yoked us together in a city of foreigners.

I don't want a cigarette now, but the ritual of smoking and some fresh air might help me find the right words. The garden is the reason behind my affection for this pub. I like its arboreal contrariness. An exotic monkey puzzle dominates the floodlit patio, its otherness highlighted by the indigenous foliage of holly bushes and fruit trees surrounding it. We take our coffees outside and stand under the electric heater. The orange light seems fake and garish against the backdrop of the holly berries, still scattered like blood blisters amongst the glossy leaves.

'No cow hides,' Andy says. Again, I take it as a positive sign – this harking back to our courtship.

'So,' he hesitates. I see the man I met, the diffidence as he turned to me, smiling, holding out the faux fur wrap. His gentleness. His father would have draped it with authority across my shoulders, would have straightened it and perhaps lifted my hair from beneath it. Andy had simply handed it to me. 'You look cold,' he'd said.

I don't feel like smoking now, but I light up, and let the cigarette burn. A city squirrel watches us from the horizontals of the monkey puzzle tree. It grips its tail in its paws and razors pointed teeth through ashy fur.

'Warm enough?'

I nod, put my cigarette to my lips, and pretend to inhale.

'So what happened?'

'Have you spoken to your father?'

The squirrel leaps from the tree to the top of the holly bush, tugs off a berry and palms it into its mouth. The berries are supposed to be poisonous.

'Tell me your version first,' Andy says.

'Version?' I feel a spike of something beneath my ribs. A sharp churning that could be anger or nerves.

'Just tell me what happened, Kate. Why you left. Why you didn't call.'

The rejected berry lands with a bloody splat on the paving and the squirrel swabs at its snout.

'Did your father tell you about the deer?' It still haunts me. The mahogany gleam of its hide in the headlights. The outline of its neck and jaw as it turned its head, the glint of its eye, and the jolt of the seatbelt between my breasts as Andy's father hit the brakes, then the flag of white as the deer disappeared into the bushes. Half a second later, the impact and the wet crunch and the windscreen blackened, and the seatbelt cutting now, and a jagged pain in my neck.

'What deer?'

It crosses my mind that Andy's bluffing, but despite his secrets, I don't think he'd do that.

'We hit a deer on the way back from dropping you off at the airport. We missed the first one, but not the second.'

Andy nods. 'They always come in pairs.'

'That's exactly what your father said.'

Andy claims he has nothing in common with his father, and that his mother is the one he takes after. But the moment I met his father I could see the similarities. Andy took me down to meet him three weeks ago. Robert, Andy's father, lived on a gated estate, full of fat detached houses fronting the sea. Most of them 1960s or 70s 'mock' something. Mock Georgian, mock Grecian villa, mock Spanish hacienda, mock Bauhaus.

'I've only been here twice.' Andy crept over the speed ramps, his body hunched forwards and his signet ring tapping nervily against the steering wheel. 'Christ, it's like Disneyland. Everywhere you look there's an architectural cliché.' He took his foot off the accelerator and stalled to a stop. 'We could make an excuse. I could say we've broken down.'

'Don't be silly.' I squeezed his knee. 'It'll be fine.'

'I haven't seen him for two years.' Andy started the engine and we crawled on, past pillars, turrets, balconies, verandahs, and thatched roofs with eyebrow windows.

'I think this is it.' He'd stopped outside a brick Georgian pile. 'Okay, let's do it.'

Andy pressed the bell and we stood huddled together under the oversized pillared porch.

There was a sense of movement, firm, measured footsteps, and the door was flung open. 'Welcome! Welcome!' Robert filled the entrance, legs wide, arms out. 'Finally the prodigal son returns!'

He was a larger, louder Andy. As if Andy were the echo, and he were the shout. Three inches taller than Andy. Broader. Deeper voiced. He was one of those men who wear their hormones on their sleeves. I could see why he and Andy clashed. He was the type of man I automatically dislike, who raises all my feminist hackles. If you dig deep you know you'll find any number of raw insecurities, yet on the surface he's all public school, rugby playing maleness. I would have taken a bet that he'd got a bloody great wine cellar and a bunch of rowing or rugby trophies tucked away at the back of some cabinet.

'No wonder he kept you a secret. You're like my wife. The same type. Andy took after her too. Slight. My colouring but Jilly's shape.' He grabbed my wrists, drew me to him, did the shoulder hug, the cheek kiss. 'Happy Christmas. Or should I say Happy New Year. Call me Robert.' He smelt of cigars and an odd scent I couldn't place.

The house was as I'd expected – a panelled hallway, and a marble reproduction fireplace with fake logs and gas flames. He gave us a tour, ending with the master bedroom. Sea view, avocado ensuite, fourposter with a mirrored ceiling. 'This is for you. I moved to the spare room when Jilly died. We had five good years here.' He winked. 'I'll leave you to unpack. Enjoy.'

'Thought we'd go for a walk. Before the light goes.' Andy was already sidling out of the room, his eyes averted from his parents' bed and the mirrored ceiling.

Outside dusk had already fallen and the landscape was losing definition. The line between the sea and the land was blurred, but you could hear the water sighing against the pebbles and just see the milky froth of the breakers.

Andy lit up a cigarette and passed it to me as we walked along the beach. 'I did warn you.'

'What do you mean? He's fine.'

'He's a frigging dinosaur. We never got on. Even when I was a kid.'

'He's missed you.' I slipped my arm through his. 'I'm glad we came. We shouldn't have left it this long. He's your dad. '

'I hate the place.'

His voice was petulant. I saw him suddenly as a child. Delicate. A mummy's boy. In Munich he was gentle and smart and arty.

Here, he looked out of place in his thin blazer and skinny jeans. He stumbled along next to me, his gait awkward on the pebbles, his pointed, leather-soled shoes slipping and his hair flopping over his eyes.

'We won't stay long.' He bent to pick up a pebble and hurled it into the water. 'Shit.' He scrubbed his hands on his jeans. 'It's covered in fucking tar.'

'Come on. Let's go back. You're shivering.' I pushed down a flare of irritation. 'You should have borrowed your Dad's coat.'

Back at the house Robert was waiting with crystal tumblers of whisky and gingers. He slung an arm around my shoulders, drew me in. 'Supper's in the Aga. Fire's on. Come and warm up.'

Andy hopped about trying to wipe tar of his shoes.

'Always was clumsy.' Robert gestured at him with his whisky glass. 'Took him ice skating as a kid. Like Bambi. That's what we called him.' He grinned and pointed to the black goo staining the tan leather of Andy's Jonhstons. 'Should have worn my wellies.'

'They're too big.' Andy threw his shoes into the utility room, his face shuttered and angry. 'Jesus. They're fucking ruined.'

Robert had made game casserole. He ladled the steaming stew onto piles of mashed potato. 'Watch out for pellets. I shot them myself.' He laughed at Andy's expression. 'That's what I do now. If you bothered to visit once in a while you'd know.' He squeezed Andy's shoulder to take away the sting of the words. 'It's a hunter's paradise here. Sea fishing on your doorstep – if you want it. But there's everything else on the Downs. We even get deer in the garden – they come across from the vineyard. I've got a freezer full. Venison, rabbit, pheasant. I butcher them myself. Saves a fortune.'

'It's delicious.' I kicked Andy's foot. 'Isn't it, Andy?'

'Yeah. Not bad.'

'Riesling. That's the trick. Expect you two drink it over in Krautland. Perfect for coq au vin. Odd that. German wine for a

French dish. But it's subtle, floral. Works with the rabbit flesh. And I always serve it with red. A decent Burgundy.' He cradled the bottle and palmed it towards Andy. 'Got a cellar full of this stuff. Some people would serve white, but I like the contrast. That's what you need. Light and shade. What d'you reckon, Katie love?'

'Works for me.'

Andy neatly sliced a mushroom, popped it into his mouth and chewed slowly. 'How come you never cooked when Mum was alive?'

'No point in having a dog and barking yourself. Jesus, just a turn of phrase, Andy. ' Robert slapped his hand on the table and leant towards Andy. 'Come on now. You know I worshipped your mother.'

Andy mellowed over supper, the food and the constant flow of Bordeaux seemed to blunt his irritation. We toasted our engagement, and talked about the wedding. Robert offered to pay. 'I've got more than enough. And your mother would have wanted me to. She'd have loved to have been involved. Hats and flowers and all the trimmings. I know how expensive it can be.'

'It's only a registry office. Nothing big.' I pressed Robert's arm. 'Thank you, but it's all sorted.'

'It's what Kate wanted. I'd have done the whole shebang.' Andy pushed his foot against mine. 'Simple, that's what you said, wasn't it love?' He was beginning to slur. 'I wanted the church thing. Big white dress.' He traced an hourglass in the air. 'You'd look gorgeous.'

I tucked my feet under my chair.

'It was hard enough to get her to marry me in the first place.'

I concentrated on scraping away the flesh from the rabbit bone.

'Three times I had to ask her.'

My tongue found a pellet. I spat it into my palm and put in on the edge of my plate.

'Said she doesn't like making promises. Didn't you, Kate?'

'Third time lucky then. Don't blame her for playing hard to get.' Robert caught my eye and smiled. 'Come on. Night's still young. Drink up.'

It was past midnight when we got to bed. I'd worried that Andy would feel uncomfortable sleeping in his parents' old room, but the alcohol had inured him to any such sensibilities. He sat in bed in his boxers, sipping his Cognac. I took the glass from his hand, put it on the bedside table, pushed him back and straddled him.

'Come on, Andy. It's the right time.' I kissed and nuzzled his chest. We'd been together for two years. We knew each other's bodies, how we fitted, what we liked. We were trying for a baby. I was wet and ready when I pulled him on top of me. But in the end it was me who couldn't shake the room's history, and I faked orgasm to draw it to a swift close. Andy slept immediately. I lay awake, hot and restless. I tried to concentrate on the ticking of my body – the gentle tugging in my ovaries – but it was drowned out by the clanking of the radiators and the muted shushing of the sea. The clouds shifted, and the moonlight flooded in, and that's when I saw our reflection in the mirror. I barely recognized us. The tangled sheets. Our pale otherness. The damp pillow beneath my buttocks. My hopefully tilted pelvis. We seemed reduced – the topography of our bodies strange and diminished. I imagined Robert, the reflection he would cast.

I awoke alone to the sound of voices outside the room. Andy's side of the bed was cold.

'Knock, knock! You decent?'

I sat up and tucked the duvet under my chin as Robert came in with a mug and a plate of toast. 'Andy said you preferred tea.'

'Sure. Thanks. What time is it?'

'Still early. But Andy's had a call from work.' Robert placed the plate on my lap. 'Plum jam. Home made. One of the partners is sick. Andy's flying back for some client meeting. Booking a flight now.' He sat on the edge of the bed and patted my leg through the duvet. 'Only twenty four hours. You're to stay here. There's a storm coming, so you can just chill, watch movies, read a book. Whatever.' His weight on the mattress tipped me towards him. I could feel the warm bulk of him next to me and the mass of him above me in the mirror.

'What d'you say, Kate? That okay? Putting up with an old man for a day?'

I eased myself sideways. 'Sure. Of course.'

We dropped Andy off at Gatwick airport later that afternoon. It was already dark when we waved him into the terminal building. The roads were waterlogged on the way back, the rain lashing at the windows and the wind tugging at the Land Rover. We hit the deer when we were nearly home. It came out of the vineyard after we'd turned off the A27. Robert had been telling me that I was only the second girl Andy had ever brought home.

'First one was his fiancée. Nice enough.' He pressed his palm briefly on my wrist. 'Not as pretty as you, of course. Longest engagement on the planet. He'd have told you about her.'

'Sure. Yeah.' I kept my voice neutral. 'How long was it again?'

'Seven years. Seven-year itch, isn't that what they say? That's when she dumped him.'

'He's mentioned her. Obviously. But not much. Seven years? Why did she leave? Was it another guy?'

'Supposedly not. Think it was timing. She wanted children and Andy wasn't ready. So he said.'

'What do you mean?'

'Nothing really. Just crossed my mind they might not have been able to. Only a thought. Honestly. A passing thought. That was all.'

Anger budded in my stomach, unfurled to the swish of the windscreen wipers and the soft click of Robert's wedding ring against the steering wheel. The first deer appeared as if I'd conjured it, then it was gone in two bounds and Robert was braking and saying they usually come in pairs. There was a shuddering jolt and the thudding mass of it against the glass. When we stopped Robert unclipped me, pressed his fingers against the back of my neck, cupped my face, checked I could turn my head, and tucked his jacket around me.

'Kate? So you hit a deer. Why did you leave? Where did you go?'

I drop my cigarette next to the burst berry and stamp it out. 'Your father brought it home and butchered it in the cellar.'

'What happened?'

I light another cigarette and shake my head. 'Nothing. It's like you said before. It's just a horrible place. I went to Mum's.'

I didn't see Robert heft the deer into the back of the Land Rover, but I breathed in its musky heat and the metallic tang of blood. The windows were wet with condensation, so we drove with them open, the storm squalling in at us both. I watched him drag it out when we got home, and carry it over his shoulder down to the basement. It was still warm, its head swinging a little over Robert's back, its eyes muted. He said he wanted to butcher it then and there, while it was still fresh. You could see the excitement in his eyes. He grabbed my face and kissed the top of my head; told me I could have the hide as a belated Christmas present. He took me into the living room, wrapped me in a tartan blanket and made me a Cognac coffee. The alcohol burned through me, my skin glowing, my fingers tingling. I turned on the television and tried to watch the news but all I could think about was what was happening below me in the cellar.

I went down bare foot. The concrete was cold and grainy against my soles. He'd left the door ajar. A spotlight threw a funnel of light over them both. The deer's head was tilted back, its throat exposed, almost coyly, like an ingénue. I watched him spread its legs, slit it open, run his fingers up inside the skin. He tugged it off like a glove, bracing the body with his foot as he hauled at the hide. That's when he turned and saw me. The skin was still in his hands; he was breathing heavily. His face was flecked with blood and blistered with sweat. I stepped forward, held open the blanket and closed my eyes. He eased me down onto the floor, his hands wet and certain, his body hot and solid. Through the basement grille, I could hear the heaving swell of the sea hammering at the shore, and smell the storm-ripped vegetation and the sweet sap of snapped wood.

In the pub garden I scribble out my cigarette. 'So what did your dad say?'

'Nothing. That you'd left. That's all.' Andy's voice is choked. He avoids my eyes, pulling off a holly leaf, examining it, pressing his finger against the spikes. 'I thought I'd lost you.'

There is a dull ache in my heart. I put my arms around him, hold him close. We are the same height. We fit together perfectly. 'I'm sorry.' His cheek is as soft as a child's. There is a pulling in my stomach, a wash of tenderness. 'It's okay. We're going to be fine. I promise.'

We agree to forget the last three weeks and to start again in Munich. I don't ask about his previous fiancée, and I don't tell him I stopped taking contraception over a year ago. I send him back inside for another coffee, and wait in the garden, beneath the monkey puzzle and the fruit trees, with their secret buds, like tightly furled wombs reaching for the sun.

Sharp As Sherbert Lemons

In hindsight the telephone box is more a trap than a hiding place. I can see the back of Tash's head and the bleached 'FU' that's beginning to grow out and mingle with the rest of her hair. It reminds me of the cress-head we planted in infant school. The one I forgot to water and which Mum had to replant because I was too scared to take it into school. I wonder if Tash had it done at the hairdresser's in town, but I can't imagine the 'FU' sitting well amongst the perms and blue rinses. Maybe it was the barbers at the top of Sydney Street, who do the skinheads from Whitehawk. I went in once to buy some gel for Dad and all the customers stared at me. They didn't turn their heads, but their eyes were all skewed towards me in the row of mirrors. I walked straight back out, with a pathetic charade of pushing up my sleeve and looking at my watch and making a sort of *umph* of surprise as if I'd just remembered I was late for something.

It's cold in the bottom of the telephone box. Despite the three broken panes it stinks of wee and damp and of the dried-up crusty pile of stuff in the corner that looks like regurgitated spaghetti hoops. The wind's picking up now, chasing wisps of dark cloud across the ashy sky and rattling gusts of icy air around my legs. They're aching from the pressure of crouching down for so long, but I can't flop onto my bottom because of the yucky floor and because getting up from a sitting position would be slower and would make me feel even more vulnerable. I can't stand up because Tash will see me. And Tash is after me, that's for sure. Everyone in the sixth form disco has said so. *Tash's looking for you,* they said, one after the other as I stumbled from the loo, through the bar, to the reception area and finally out into the safety of the cold night air. It's only 11.00 and I'm not getting picked up for another hour. I lied to my parents about the finish time so I could spend longer with Simon. Where is Simon? He should be looking for me by now. We've only been going out for a fortnight, but he really likes me. He'll be wondering where I am.

Tash is standing on the youth centre steps, only a few yards from the phone box. One hand's fisting her hip and the other's at her ear and she's yacking into her mobile. The youth club's not properly sound-proofed and the bass notes are escaping into the night in tinny blasts, making it impossible to hear what she's saying. Her mouth's gupping, and every now and again she gives a sharp nod of her head, but you can see her heart's not really in the conversation because all the while she's turning in a slow circle, scanning the area. I know what the phrase 'eyes peeled' means now. Even from the bottom of the phone box, in the on-off-moonlight as the clouds slice across the sky, Tash's eyes look raw and sharp and focused. I concentrate on breathing. I draw the cold, phone-box air in slowly, and out again. In and out. Stay calm. You'd think if you were going to vandalise a phone box you'd wreck the light, but they've left that alone. Everything else has been smashed or ripped or broken, but the light's survived. The cover's chipped and it's full of the carcasses of winged things that were lured by the brightness, but in the winter dusk it's still shining like a beacon. If I move an inch Tash will see me.

Tash's brother's in borstal. GBH. Bottled some bloke in The Seahorse for chatting up his girlfriend. Tash is just as tough. She reminds me of a rescue cat we used to have. A skinny tabby thing with huge orange eyes that beat the crap out of our other two cats and would scratch and spit and lunge at you like a demon if you went near it. It got run over in the end. Tash is just as skinny and she constantly looks like she's been in a fight. Half the time she comes into school with a black eye or a fat lip. But despite all that Simon went out with her. No one could understand why, although I guess she used to be pretty, in a pale, edgy, Amy Winehouse kind of way, but still, Simon was always out of her league.

Everyone fancies Simon, with his surfy-lemon-hair, and ripped chest. He plays footie for the A-team, and he's got a car. He went out with Tash long-term. But he chucked her a month ago. On Facebook. Which was horrible. He admitted that. Said it wasn't kind. 'I had to,' he said, 'she wouldn't get the message. I had to do something drastic.' I wasn't really listening properly because he was running his fingers through my hair. He's obsessed with my hair, he grabs fistfuls of it and holds it up to his nose, then whispers his fingertips along the nape of my neck so my stomach goes liquid and I feel wet and slack all over. When he kisses me I dissolve and fizz inside like those flying saucer sweets I used to get from the corner shop.

That's where I used to see Tash. Years ago when we were at infant school. It was on our way home. I can still see her with those long caramel plaits and that plastic 'My Little Pony' bag over her shoulder. I was jealous of that bag, shiny and bright and gobstopper pink. I was desperate for one but when I asked Mum she just laughed and said it wasn't 'appropriate' for school.

They're playing the slow numbers now. Katie Perry's *The one that got away*. I imagine the notes jiggling through the gaps in the doors and windows. The crotchets and quavers spiralling out, sauntering, careless, adagissimo, until they're grabbed by the wind and tugged up and away. Tash is off the phone and she's got her hand up to her forehead to screen her eyes from the flood-lights on the youth centre roof. She makes me think of some tacky mime artist trying to imitate a sailor. A bubble of nervy laughter swells up in my throat. My legs are burning; pins and needles are pricking the balls of my feet. I grab the yellow pages' shelf and pull myself up a few inches to release the pressure on my thighs. Tash is rubbing a hand across the back of her head. It's probably still a novelty, the feeling of shorn hair. She had it cut after Simon chucked her. I imagine her marching into the barbers, asking for a 'number one' or 'number two' or whatever it's called. The FU has been shaved in a few inches above the nape of her neck and you can still see her skin glinting through, white as chicken meat. I ease myself up another foot. And that's when Tash turns and sees me. Her hands drop to her sides and she's coming over in big, purposeful strides and it's too late to try and get out and make a run for it.

My legs are mush and my heart feels like it's trying to smash its way out of my body. Then Tash is at the door. The stupid thing is, the phone booth shouldn't even be here. It's a relic. The club auctioned it off last week. Some weirdo collector should have taken it away by now. Orchids, that's what they said he was going to use if for. Some kind of retro greenhouse. He was planning to stick in a heater and a humidifier to keep the flowers safe and cosy. It sent shivers down my spine when I heard about it. I imagined the plants thrusting and pushing against the glass as he stroked and snipped and sprayed.

It was a crazy place to hide. Now I'm trapped. I should have just gone home. Or found Simon. He'd have looked after me. He's old-fashioned like that. He's walked me to and from school every day since he asked me out. He waits for me in the morning outside my house and outside my classroom every afternoon at four.

'You're Freya, right?'

As I stand up a swirl of nausea hits the back of my throat. I manage to nod.

'Freya?' It's a shout. Simon. Finally. I can see him in silhouette, at the club entrance. His shadow spills out, long and thin and black as liquorice over the steps and the gravel.

'You're shagging Simon, right?' Tasha's face is squashed and distorted against the glass.

I hook my fingers through one of the broken panes and hold the door shut. 'Simon's over there. He's coming.'

Tash digs in her shorts' pocket. Pulls something out. There's a dull click and the light glints on the blade.

Her face is still and porridge-pale through the scratched glass of the kiosk door.

Simon's looking around. 'Freya! You okay?'

I step back and the bars of the booth dig into my spine. 'Simon's coming.'

Tash opens her mouth and closes it and clears her throat. When she speaks her voice is low and intense. 'Dump him.'

I force myself to hold her gaze. Don't blink. I concentrate on the faint sulphurous bruise around her left eye.

Behind her shoulder I can see Simon.

'You bought me some sherbet lemons once.' I say. The memory's come out of nowhere. I'd lost my purse or maybe forgotten my money. I remember standing in the shop. The woman behind the counter shaking her head and drawing back the paper bag of sweets. Tash next to me, reaching into her pink pony bag. 'I'll pay.'

'Do you remember?' I swallow, and try and keep my voice level. 'At infant school. In the corner shop. You paid for my sweets.'

Tash shrugs, an echo of the gesture she made all those years ago when I'd thanked her. 'Whatever he's said, it's not love.'

'He's coming.'

'I left him. You didn't know that, did you? He put the thing on Facebook afterwards.'

'What d'you want?' My voice is high and brittle.

Tash's hand is swinging at her side, the knife tapping softly against the glass. 'Mum said I was well rid.'

There's a stillness to her face now. I can't tell whether she's holding back anger or tears.

'What d'you want?'

She shrugs again. 'Dunno. I was curious. That's all.' She lifts up her top. In the weak, fly-filtered light I see a funny pattern of little circles across her stomach, like milky petals, where the flesh is white and shiny and smooth. 'Does he do it to you?' She runs her fingers across the tiny scars. 'Does he do this?'

My gut churns. I shake my head. She was always weird. Mum was right. I look away and concentrate on the grubby bubblegum heart stuck to the corner of the pane. 'He's coming.'

Tash's breath is misting the glass. 'Does he like your hair? He loved mine.'

And then Simon's here, looming up out of the dark behind her. 'Go home, Tash.' His voice is calm and flat and controlled. She whips round and flails at him with the knife. He shoves her away, grabs her wrist and grabs the knife. She steps back and stumbles and crumples up like a coke can.

'Go home, Tash.' He pulls open the door. 'Sorry Freya. It's alright, I've got you now.' He pulls me into his arms, holds me tight and safe and warm against the cage of his chest. 'You're shaking. You don't want to believe a word she says. You know that, don't you? She's full of crap.'

My cheek's pressed against his jumper. I breathe in his scent of cigarettes and aftershave and washing powder.

'Look.' He pushes me gently away and holds out Tash's knife. 'It's just a Swiss Army thing. She didn't even get the blade out.' He shoves his hand through his hair and gives a grunt of laughter. 'It's the tweezers. Maybe she wanted to pluck your eyebrows.'

I force out a smile. The knife's the same gobstopper pink as the bag she used to have. Simon lifts my chin and looks me straight in the eyes. 'She used it to cut herself. I felt sorry for her. That's why I stayed so long. She's not right.' He taps his head then leans in to kiss me. His lips are soft and insistent but there's something different about it this time. Beneath the sweet fizzing of flying saucers there's the sharp, acidic tang of lemon. I remember then, running home from the corner shop that day, sucking the sherbet lemon so hard it cut my tongue. And afterwards the salt-sweet taste in my mouth, and Mum's irritation when I told her who'd given me the money.

'I was so worried.' He pulls me closer, smoothing my hair in long, firm strokes, from the top of my head to my waist. 'She talks crap. You know that? What did she say?'

'Nothing.' I lift my head from his shoulder and watch Tash walking away. One hand is fisting at her tears, the other is moving up and down over the soft bristles of her crewcut.

'It's okay, Freya. I've got you.'

I close my eyes and press my face against Simon's chest, but I can still see Tash's outline, imprinted on my retina, sharp and shining bright.

CLIPPING KIKI

When I find the feather I'm transported back to last summer. It's the summer of the parrot and the heatwave; the year the stream at the Shepherd and Dog dries up, Sidney Street re-soles my flip-flops with tar, and the eye-aching yellow of the rapeseed field up at Dewer's farm shrivels to tobacco brown. It is the summer of my GCSEs, and my first job. And Kiki.

We get the letter on a Tuesday. The postman stands at the door swabbing his forehead with the back of his wrist and scratching at the stiff fabric of his shorts. As he hands me the envelope a droplet of sweat balloons on the pale blue paper. He used to go to my school. He was a couple of years above me. He was cool. Good looking. Went out with Candy Marshall and got spotted by a scout from Millwall. Now he's our postman. He seems more awkward than usual in his summer uniform. Kind of exposed, as if his knees and shins are unused to such freedom.

He hitches up his bag. 'Survived the exams then?'

The pale blotchiness of his legs spikes a memory of an undercooked pastry dish I made in year seven. 'Just.' I examine the envelope. Handwritten. The postmark is too smudged to give anything away.

'You'll do great, Freya. Better than me. You won that English prize, didn't you?'

I shrug and smile, and he thumbs away a teardrop of sweat and wiggles crossed fingers at me. When he walks back up the path, his shadow skirts the overflowing recycling bin, but he doesn't glance down. I like Alex.

We never get this sort of letter. I click the kettle on, and stand in the buzzing cool of the fridge, staring at the envelope. The writing is fat and loopy, with a left slant, like Mum's. When I hold it to my nose I get a waft of damp paper and the sweet staleness of Alex's BO. Then Mum comes down, showered and dressed, and I know it's going to be a good day.

We're out of tea, so I make her a cup with my old teabag. We sit down together and she turns the envelope over a couple of times, props it against her mug and tells me who it's from.

'Lisa.'

'Right.'

'Your aunt. Remember?'

'Not really. You going to open it?'

She palms up her hair and rocks back on the hind legs of the chair. 'You know. My sister.'

'Shall I?' I finger it open, tearing the envelope a little as I pull out the folded slip of paper. 'Here.'

'You read it.'

There's a couple of opening platitudes and then: *Mum wanted you to have Kiki, so can you come and get him? We keep him caged now – he bit me the other day. If you don't want him, we'll put him on Ebay.*

'Who's Kiki?' For a second I picture some half-brother, locked away, slobbering in a gothic attic.

'Our parrot.' She takes the letter. 'He was mine. When I was about your age. Mine and Lisa's. He liked me best.' She palms out the paper and lights up a cigarette. 'Made a change.'

'But Gran died years ago.'

'Two.' She tilts her head and gups out a smoke ring. 'I didn't hang around after the funeral.' She bats away the little circle of smoke. 'Shall we go and get him?'

119

'Really?' I search her face. 'D'you mean it?'

'Sure.'

'When?'

'Now.' She shoves back her chair. 'Right now.'

'What about Clemmie?'

'We'll be back in time to pick her up.' She's up and laughing and scribbling out her cigarette in the sink. 'Come on.' She runs the tap on the butt and points out of the window. 'He's an African Grey. He used to love this weather. We let him outside in the summer. He talks. Loads.' She puts on a funny voice. *'Pieces of eight, pieces of eight!'* and then she hugs me and her breath smells of toothpaste and even her body seems less sharp than usual.

In the end I don't go. Chris next door takes Mum. He's been pensioned off early from the Post Office because of a dodgy back, but he still has an old PO van and he delivers for the mail order companies. Next and La Redoute and stuff. He has a van-full, so there's no room for me, but I wave them off. Mum all buzzy and shiny and Chris squatting next to her like Gloin, with his ashy beard tossed over one shoulder and a straining Deff Leppard tee-shirt pressing against the bottom of the steering wheel.

I run the vacuum round and sit in the garden for a bit with a Steinbeck from next year's reading list, but I can't concentrate, so I stick Mum's empties in a couple of carriers and took them to down to the recycling opposite the Spar. I feed them through the rubber mouth one by one and listen to them crash as they hit the bottom. I buy teabags and fishfingers then go down early to meet Clemmie. They surge out in a tide of blue, the girls giggling and clutching each other; the boys' rugby-tackling, arm-locking and knuckling heads. Clemmie's different. She looks older than nine. She comes out alone, eyes down, quiet and concentrated. Even the way she walks is careful, each step neat and focused. She's like that with her homework too, everything underlined and colour-coded and organized.

I tell her about the parrot. 'An African Grey. He's called Kiki after the one in the Enid Blyton books. You know, the ones Mum read us.'

She shrugs. 'Not to me. She never read to me.'

I take her bag. 'You were probably too little to remember.'

When we get home they're back. A massive domed cage is sitting on the kitchen table, the bars shining in the sunlight. Chris and Mum are standing there, staring at it. Chris is pulling at his beard like he's milking a cow, and Mum has an unlit ciggie stuck to her bottom lip.

The bird's smaller than I imagined. And calling him 'grey' is a ridiculous over-simplification. He's like the examples of pencil shading techniques Clem's got in her art book. The base of his wings are bruised storm-cloud black, then he fades from school-uniform to smoke to pewter to ash. The feathers on his stomach are the palest moonshine. Everything about him is curved. His face is covered with frills of tiny, layered, oval feathers, each one lined with a perfect rim of white. His beak is a fat, black arc.

'His tail looks as if it's been put on the wrong bird.'

Clem's right. His tail is like a last minute joke, or an act of repentance. It's a bright post-box red.

'Hello.' I move closer and he puts his head on one side. You can see from his eyes that he's clever. He sits on his perch, with his pupils dilating and shrinking, watching me right back.

Clem asks if our aunt will miss him, and whether she'll come down and visit. Mum makes a face and says she doubts it and that Lisa has her head stuck too far up her own arse to bother with a parrot or a sister or her nieces. Then she claps her hands. 'We ought to have a drink to celebrate. Toast his arrival. And the end of your exams, Freya. We never did that did we?'

Clemmie and I exchange glances. Chris says, 'Good idea, I'm parched.' He fills the kettle, I get the tea, and Clem rinses out the mugs. The silence mushrooms out, fat and weighty, and then Mum says, 'Jesus,' grabs herself a glass and is walking towards the cupboard under the stairs when a voice chimes out: *Two Sugars! Two Sugars!*

Mum stops, and Chris lets out a cough of laughter. Mum's lips twitch, and Clem starts giggling. Chris nips next door for some biscuits and we sit around the table like a proper family, dunking and drinking and staring at Kiki who's holding half a digestive in his claw as if he's human.

We all fall in love with him that summer. I'm used to being the first one up, coming into a silent kitchen and tidying up the empties, but now, every morning he's waiting for me, clinging to the bars and telling me to put the kettle on. When we go to the back door he screeches goodbye; he tells Mum to tidy her room and eat her greens. He has a Northern accent and Mum says it's Gran's and it's like a voice from the bloody grave. But I can tell she likes it. He plays football on the kitchen floor, his tail wagging from side to side as he swaggers flat-footed after a marble.

Clem doesn't care any more when her friends text holiday photos. She sends back pictures of Kiki. They asks what he's like and she says 'complicated'. She's got it right as usual.

He's a fickle bird. He only dunks his biscuits in very sweet tea, and he'll dance to Hip-Hop but he hates Garage. Sometimes he fluffs himself up, each layer of feathers fat with air and he lets you pick him up and cuddle him. Other times he's mean and thin, his feathers drawn in tight against his body, all sharp and wild. He screeches and snakes his head so that we have to throw a blanket over his cage to shut him up. Sometimes he sulks in the corner, silent and stony. I wonder if he's thinking of Africa and sticky, forest-filtered sunshine and flocks of pewter and scarlet.

'Born in a cage,' Mum said. 'In Bradford.'

'He can still dream,' I say.

He likes us all, but Mum's his favourite. She spends more time downstairs now. He crouches on her wrist, beside himself with love. His whole body trembles, his wings curve around her hand, and he croons, his beak half open, his fat black tongue shivering. He sways up and down and side to side, stretching and pumping. If Mum holds him to her face, he rubs against her cheek and regurgitates food for her, his throat pulsing and his tongue shunting it to the edge of his beak.

Most days Chris came over with jugs of iced tea. He milks his beard and tells us parrot jokes: *What do you get when you cross a parrot and a centipede? A walkie-talkie.* We sit in the garden with Kiki on top of his cage or on our shoulders. I read, Clem draws pictures of Kiki, and Mum pots up geraniums. Day after day the only clouds on an endless, forget-me-not sky, are the vapour trail kisses of distant planes.

Alex brings the second letter a week after Kiki arrives. He strides up the path, red-shinned, swiping the back of his neck, nodding approval at the geraniums. 'One for you Freya.' He stretches out his arm to pass it to me, revealing the sweat-patches two-toning his shirt. 'Hot enough for you? Looks like it might last.'

A holiday job at the Metropole down on Brighton seafront. I can't believe my luck. I start the next day. They give me a uniform and train me up for silver service, taking me on for breakfast and lunch shifts. Seven quid an hour plus tips. I even enjoy the early mornings: the empty bus, the skimmed-milk-translucence of the sky, the stillness of the Brighton streets, the softness of the briny air. I bring home croissants, neat little pots of jam and foiled rectangles of butter. They say they'll keep me on at the weekends when I'm in the sixth form. I open an account at the TSB and start saving for university.

In between shifts I go down to the beach with a bag of books from the A-level syllabus. When I'm bored with reading I look for cuttle fish. You find them at the flotsam line, gleaming chalkily amongst the rotting seaweed, the driftwood and the rubbish. Curved and white, exfoliated smooth and clean. They're Kiki's favourite. He cost nothing really. Sunflower seeds from the market, freebie newspapers for the bottom of his cage, and bread and croissants from work. I like watching him eating the seeds, one at a time, cracking the shell first, then teasing out the kernel with his fat black tongue.

By the end of July we can't remember what cold weather feels like. The parks and verges are as dry as tobacco, and along our street the leaves hang from the plane trees like they've given up. I get home one day to find Mum in the garden, standing next to Kiki's cage, staring up at the empty sky.

'He just took off.' She shakes her head. 'Bounced on top of the cage a couple of times.' She swipes her hands on her denim buttocks. 'Thought he was laying an egg. Then he just spread his wings and went.'

An empty bottle rolls on the grass and I can smell the wine on her breath.

'Remember when we took Clem's stabilisers off? And you gave her a push, and then she just kept going? Not even a wobble? That's what he was like. As if he'd done it forever. Straight towards the sea. Reckon he was heading for Africa. Can't say I blame him.' She kicks the cage lightly. 'That's why I didn't want him. Can't stand caged things. Not right.' She picks up the bottle, shakes it. 'Don't look so worried. He didn't get far. Ted phoned – from the offie. He's found him.'

Kiki's in a tree opposite the off-licence, surrounded by a flock of sparrows. Ted, the owner, brings out a step-ladder and a bag of prawn cocktail crisps to coax him down. Afterwards Clemmie and I take him to the vets. It needs two of them, both gloved-up, Kiki wrapped in a towel. 'Like cutting hair,' the vet says as he concertinas the wing.

'Like Samson.' Clemmie says.

'Nice bird. I like African Greys. All embers and ash.' The vet starts clipping. 'Just the ten primary ones. That'll fix him.'

It makes me think of *The Wide Sargasso Sea* from next year's reading list. It's a weird book. The heroine's parrot is burnt alive – fluttering and flaming to its death. Rhys didn't need to kill it. The vet points to one of the smaller feathers, 'That's new, a pin one. That'll bleed. That's what you avoid if you're doing it yourself.'

Clemmie shakes her head. 'Not me. I'd rather he flew away.'

'Don't worry.' The vet clips carefully through the cartilage, 'Won't notice a thing. Born in captivity. They don't know any better.'

The third letter is my GCSE results. Alex is still in shorts and shirt. Legs finally tanned. He keeps his eyes straight ahead now, avoiding the wilting geraniums and the recycling. 'Good luck, Freya.'

My hands are sweating more than his and my throat's drier than the grass. But they aren't bad at all. More than enough for me to do the A-levels I want. University seems almost real. When I tell Mum she gets dressed and comes downstairs. She raps me on the head. 'You sure you're my daughter?'

Kiki plays football with the screwed-up envelope and Chris cooks us spag bol and we drink iced tea and google universities that are close enough for me to come home at the weekends to check on Clem and Mum. At the hotel a couple of waitresses take me clubbing. They're both students, home for the holidays. They tell me about Freshers week, and the lecture halls, the weird professors, and the communal kitchens and how everyone nicks each other's food. I sit there listening to them all night, sipping Bacardi Breezers. When the holidays finish the summer limps on for a bit even when we go back to school. I like the freedom of sixth form. No uniform and no science or maths. My English teacher takes a few of us to a seminar at Southampton University. I sneak off to the library and sit at one of desks. It would be perfect there – close to the sea, and close enough to keep an eye on Clem and Mum still.

There is no finite end to the heatwave, no grand storm, it just gets cooler and the milkiness of the early morning sky is more full-fat than skimmed, and it stays that colour all day. One morning I wake up and the windows are blistered with rain drops. Kiki misses Clem and me when we're at school, or maybe just misses being outside. He screeches more and speaks less. Most days the blanket's over his cage when I get home. If I take it off he starts up and Mum chucks cigarette butts at him and rams the heel of her hand against her head.

One day I arrive back from school to find an empty space in the kitchen. Mum's in bed watching 'Come Dine'. She holds out her arms, shrugging, her tan still dark against the cream duvet cover.

'Chill out, Freya. Sold him to the offie. Better off there. They like bustle. Don't they? Sociable. Like me. Not like you two.'

He does seem happy. Ted says he's good for business. If someone buys red wine Kiki shrieks out 'Bordeaux' and if it's white he yells 'Sauvignon.' I give Ted the tin I keep Kiki's sunflower seeds in, the one that's the same colour as his tail, and I tell him the best place to find cuttle fish. Clem won't go. Says she wants to remember him the way he was.

In October and November it seems to rain every day, as if we're being punished for the summer. The sky is Kiki-grey. Mum's going through a bad patch again. Even Chris has given up on her. I juggle shopping and cooking and homework and weekend shifts at the hotel. I finally go to see Kiki in the Christmas holidays and everything's changed. Ted's gone. The off licence has become a 'cave'. All glass shelves, low lights, champagne bottles and pictures of neat vineyards with French writing. A bloke in Diesel jeans and a linen shirt glances up from his Mac. 'Can I help you?'

I gesture to the walls. 'It's very grey.'

He looks me up and down, 'If you want alcohol I'll need to see your ID.'

'Where's the other guy? Ted?'

'Bought him out. He couldn't compete with the new Tesco Metro.'

'What about the parrot?'

'RSPCA took him.'

I find Kiki's red tin in the skip out the back, along with a Farrow and Ball colour chart. There are neat little crosses next to some of the greys.

That was over a year ago. Sixth form didn't work out, but I'm front of house at The Metropole now. I've got a suit (good cut, lightweight, fully lined), I get free food and I can live at home, keep an eye on Clem and help her with her homework. She wants to be an architect. She'll make it. She was always more focused than me. I found her old sketches of Kiki this morning. There was a tiny feather stuck to one of the pages, one of the soft, moonshine ones. Clem's captured him perfectly, the curves and the layered, brindled shadows. I almost expected to hear him speak, or to fly off the page. I never found out where he went to, but I like to think he grew his wings again, and snuck on board a ship bound for Africa. I imagine him amidst a flock of African Greys, flying through the warmth and colour of a rainforest. When I'm at work I still go down to the beach in between my shifts. It's just muscle memory I guess, but sometimes I find myself stooping to pick up the curved skeleton of a cuttle fish and before I know it, I've slipped it into my pocket.

Dissolving

The guard holds the white cube between his finger and thumb. He's the one who smokes menthols, who hawks up his phlegm so violently he sounds like he's going to choke. In the gloom of the cell I can't make it out. I think it's a dice, and then, when I see what it is I doubt myself. He clears his throat, bangs a fist against his chest, shoves out his chin and gobs onto the dirt floor.

'Here.' There's the damp weight of him against my shoulder, the flabby give of his stomach and a waft of mint and sweat. He pulls me away from the wall and I feel the soft scrape of his nails on my palm as he pushes it into my hand.

I identify it by touch – a sugar lump.

I think of Mrs Shepherd. Holmbush infant school. Delivering the registers with Graham Streader. Our fingertips leave moist prints on the coloured covers. One per class. The teacher's looking up, smiling, holding out a hand; coming to meet us in a waft of chalk and perfume. 'Thank you Graham, thank you Michael.' Mrs Shepherd smelled of parma violets; she had a giant screw-top jar of blurred-edged-sugar-lumps. She let us ram our hands in, pull one out and stuff it in our mouths. There'll be a rule against that kind of thing now, health and safety or something. We'd run across to the prefab huts, breath steaming the air, the second cube safe in our pockets, saved for break-time, to have with the milk. Bottles clinking, blue straws. Everyone else not being able to get enough of the stuff, but me hating the warm, rancid creaminess, and sticking my sugar lump behind my front teeth and sucking the milk through it.

'Did he give you one too?'

He hasn't spoken before. I didn't know whether he was asleep or unconscious or dead when they brought me in this morning. I recognised him instantly from his shirt. He was curled up, a human-shaped husk in the corner of the room. I recognised the floral fabric. A blue that was once azure but is now a grubby indigo. You can hardly make out the swallows and daisies. He worked on the same floor as me. He was there when they took us. Afterwards we were moved on and kept apart. They brought us together again as a group once, a few weeks ago, to make a video. One of the journalists read from a script. I knew him vaguely. He was from Solihull. Played golf. He was the type of man my dad would have been proud of – the sheet of paper quivered, but the golfer kept his voice steady and his shoulders back. Solid. I've not seen him since.

The man on the floor is a foreigner. European. Slight, effeminate, immaculate and camp. Was all those things. Odd he should have lasted this long. Perhaps he's been dishing out favours. It seems churlish not to answer him now. 'Yeah, he did.' I say.

'A sugar lump. What the fuck's that about?'

When I've deciphered his words through his accent, broken teeth and swollen lips I shrug. 'It means it's our turn.'

'Another video?'

'No.'

He looks at me. I see him moving out of the corner of my eye, twisting on his feet and backside to face me. It makes me feel uncomfortable. This isn't the place people look at each other. The guards are careful to avoid eye contact. His shoulders start to shake and he makes a wheezing, choking sound. At first I think he's crying, but it's laughter.

'Isn't it supposed to be a cigarette? Executioner's last gift?'

I shrug.

'Would have liked a ciggie. Slave to the weed, me.'

A phrase my Dad used. 'Never be a slave to the weed, boy.' I can still see him. Rolling his own, finger-tipping the tobacco onto the little rizla sheet, running the tip of his tongue along the edge, and tucking in the stray ends with the end of a match. The phrase sounds anachronistic here, in this place, with this man's accent. 'I don't smoke.'

He shuffles towards me. 'What was the point? We can't fucking eat them.'

He's right. Our hands are tied behind our backs, the grainy cube squeezed tight in our palms.

'We could stick em up our arses.'

I smile and my jaw hurts and something splits open in the corner of my mouth. 'Could do.' I clench my fist tighter to feel the shape of it. The sharp edges crumble as I squeeze. I used to know a girl in junior school who had a horse. She wore her hair in a high shiny pony-tail. When she trotted both tails used to swing and bounce in time. She'd feed it sugar lumps and I'd watch its tongue on the skin of her palm and I'd get a hard-on. We went out for a while, but it didn't last. Even Dad said I was punching above my weight.

'They're leaving.'

His accent could be Italian or Spanish. Something sing-song.

'Most of them have gone already.'

All morning there have been the sounds of departure. Shouts, truck doors slamming, the clatter of cans, the slap of folding canvas, engines revving and the spit of sand from accelerating tyres. And gun shots.

'We're the last.'

There were sixteen of us at one time. Five from my department. We usually ate in the canteen but it was someone's birthday that day, so we went to the mall for lunch. I didn't even know his name, the guy whose birthday it was. Last week the menthol guard told me the others were dead.

'They might take us? They could still use us, right? For an exchange? Why else would they keep us this long?'

He reminds me suddenly of my father. The deliberate blindness. And physically. The thinness. The bones of his face look like they're trying to push through his skin. It spikes a memory of Dad at the end. I remember the shock of him in his hospital gown. How diminished he seemed. He was always such a big, explosive man. A pint drinker. A three-sugars-in-his-tea man. A difficult-to-live-up-to man. A don't darken my doorstep again man. The type of man who would call this foreigner a chutney chaser, a shirt lifter. At the hospital I wasn't sure he'd agree to see me, but he beckoned me into his private room. Hospital's a leveller, son, he said. He was propped upright against his pillows, ramrod straight. He was always like that – clear in his views, sharp and crystalline. There was never any giving way. No crumbling. No dissolving. He was a performer, my dad, even at the end he was acting. The 'son' was for the pretty nurse. If he'd had the energy he'd have clapped me on the shoulder and winked at her. 'Never Say Die eh?'

'You're the artist aren't you?'

'Engineer.'

My cellmate shakes his head. 'You always had a sketch pad. I used to see you drawing in the canteen.'

He doesn't seem so camp now. That irritating ebullience has gone. He used to watch me from a distance. He'd stand and stare in his buttoned-up floral shirts and narrow jeans and pointed, polished shoes. He'd approach me from an angle. Would meander past, trailing his fingers along the back of my chair.

'I used to draw a bit. I'm married. Pictures of my wife.' Lately I worry that I can no longer draw her from memory. When I try to picture her face it dissolves and distorts.

Outside there's a watery cough, a rasp of movement, the jangle of keys. The guard will have taken the last drag from the butt of his cigarette, will be crushing it out between thumb and forefinger, and will be chucking it on the pile by the wall.

'Here.'

My cellmate has levered himself up and is kneeling with his back to me, his tied hands pushed up towards my face. 'Take it.' His fingers tremble. They're black with dirt and blood. The sugar lump gleams white against his curled palm. He jiggles it up and down. 'Quick.'

I'm sitting cross-legged, leaning against the wall. I shake my head but he's facing away from me. He came this close to me once in a bar. It was a departmental night out. I'd got separated from my colleagues and he found me, or followed me. He pulled up a stool, and bought me a *Tusker*, sliding it along the sticky bar. He was so close I could smell the leather of his jacket and the spice of his after-shave. His knee-cap was pressed against my thigh. He touched my wrist when I took the bottle, and looked me straight in the eyes. 'You don't fool me,' he said, swirling his fingertips along the inside of my arm. I punched him off his stool.

'Please.' his voice breaks.

I still remember the feel of his long, slim fingers against my skin.

There's the grate of the key in the lock. The sound of bolts being drawn.

I feel hot and prickly. 'He's coming. Get up.'

The door bangs open. The sun pours in, as smooth and sweet as lager. A gust of wind eddies the dirt floor. Anthony is still on his knees. I'm worried he'll cry. He looks up at the guard standing in the doorway and he laughs. 'Weather for drying.' he says in his Italian accent.

Weather for drying. I see Mum with a basket of washing and the tips of her slippered feet beneath the folds of cotton as she pegs out the sheets.

'What you say?' The guard scowls and scratches his groin.

Something that feels like a laugh bubbles up in my chest. 'How d'you know those phrases? Where did you learn them?'

'Everywhere. I lived with a boxer in Lincoln once. Six years. Now take the fucking sugar.'

I get onto my knees, spread my legs for balance, lean forward, push my face into his hand, feel the rasp of his finger nails against my lips and then the square of sugar shoved into my dry mouth.

'Now me. Quick.'

The guard is motionless in the doorway.

I draw up one leg, fold my chest forward, grunt and push up from the other toe. I'm up on both feet, swaying. My cellmate is on his knees again, shuffling behind me. I open my hand, and hold it steady. There is the damp huff of breath, then the weight and warmth of his lips and I remember the pressure of Graham's lips on mine in the geography hut and the sticky, rising swell of pleasure before I hit him so hard his nose cracked.

The guard is coughing and thumping his chest. 'Out.'

I keep my tongue still, holding the cube against the side of my cheek. We had the polio vaccine on a sugar cube. The nurse squirting it on, the gentle swell of her blue uniform against the shiny, complicated buckle of her navy belt, her fingers cupping my chin and the soft weight of her hand on my head and then the sugar dissolving on my tongue.

'Time.' The guard gestures with his chin.

He supports us both as we come squinting and shivering into the glare. We stumble like boys in a three-legged race. School sports day, Graham's calf and thigh against mine. They call it the bear sun this time of year. There's no warmth in the brightness. Every country has its colour. Here it's sand – the low lemon sun, the dusty ground, the pale buildings, the scattered handful of tan goats, the beige canvas trucks. I try to picture the green of home, the soft Sussex sun on the field behind my parents' house where I used to lie hidden in the grass as a boy, chewing the sap from stalks, waiting for the farmer to drive the sheep in, the herd milling around me like grounded clouds.

There are half a dozen of them left, in desert camouflage, cradling machine guns. One is holding up a video camera. They fall silent when they see us.

The menthol guard shoves us onto our knees and we kneel in the dirt, eyes closed against the brightness. Our shoulders touch and steady against each other. I feel the shivering warmth of him through his shirt. We turn to look at each other. He smiles. 'My name's Anthony.'

'I know.' I say.

'No hoods.' His teeth are chattering. 'Reckon we'll be on Youtube?'

There's the clunk and metallic rattle of chambers being loaded. I press closer to him and work the cube between my teeth. I focus on his eyes. They are a deep blue, the only real colour in this beige faded landscape. I think of the blue of a summer Sussex sky. As they fire I bite down and the cube dissolves, my mouth flooding with its sweetness.

ACKNOWLEDGEMENTS

My thanks to Jacqui Rochford, Val Evans, Stephanie Norgate, Jane Rusbridge and Alison Macleod for their excellent editing advice. And to Tim, James and Saskia for their support and encouragement.

'Llama Sutra'
first published on Ink Tears website, 2013, and broadcast on Radio 4, 2013

'Falafal'
first published in *The New Writer Magazine*, July 2011

'After Ever After'
first published in *Structo Magazine*, February 2014

'Baking Blind'
first published in the *Bristol Prize Anthology,* 2011

'The Singing Fish'
first published in the *Cinnamon Press Anthology: Jericho*, 2012

'After the Flood'
first published in the *Bristol Prize Anthology,* 2012

'Suicide Bomber'
first published in *Unthology 4* in 2013

'Marissa's Bike'
first published in *Prole Magazine,* 2015

'Peacock Girl'
first published in the *Rubery Prize Anthology*, 2012

'Dissolving'
first published in *Prole Magazine,* 2016

'Clipping Kiki'
first published in *Artificium*, 2016

'Silent as Storks'
shortlisted for the 2016 *Royal Academy Pin Drop Award*

WHEN PLANETS SLIP THEIR TRACKS
by Joanna Campbell

Tracing the fragile paths of people who desperately want to belong, Campbell catches her characters in the moment where they find themselves floundering. These are characters at the edge of their endurance, experiencing the moment when life threatens to tip out of their control. With a light comic flair, Campbell follows them through the twists and turns of their experiences. We see extraordinary events within mundane lives, and Campbell shatters your expectations in the award-winning stories that make up this collection. She beautifully captures the moment of implosion – a lame girl's friends disappear on a bleak mountain, a schoolboy nurses a doll during a lesson, a babysitter is caught in her own web of lies, a mother watches her pram sink in the river. Campbell makes you look at the world with a sharper eye, allowing you to see pictures in the flames, or faces in knots of wood. These stories are about people like us, carefully threading parts of their lives into a sequence, as though they were pearls on string. We meet them just as the thread is cut, scattering everything they know, and share their trials as they struggle to recover.

"Joanna Campbell's range and scope as a writer is breathtaking. These stories capture the breadth of her unique talent in a collection of unforgettable stories."
Joe Melia, Bristol Short Story Prize

BOYFRIENDS
by Bonnie West

In her debut collection, Bonnie West transforms everyday experiences into events that are complex, sometimes heart wrenching, and frequently unexpected. The collection includes stories of teenagers with an unabashed naiveté and contagious belief that they are indeed invincible; and stories of adults who are not so unlike their teenage counterparts as they follow their hearts into compromising positions. As perceptive and observant as West's characters are, they often over-estimate their knowledge, sharing a degree of honesty even when they delude themselves. A woman falling in love with a chicken, an angry pathologist, or a ghost at the edge of the woods seem unlikely scenarios, but as we read these stories we come to believe anything is possible. Throughout the collection, West's observations are piercing, irreverent, and often very funny.

"Brilliant stories that zing with humor and then break your heart – until you laugh out loud again."
                    Robin Black, author *If I Loved You I Would Tell You This*